Bears in the Punch Bowl and Other Stories

Kent Robinson

ISBN: 1-4140-3646-9 (electronic)
ISBN: 1-4140-3644-2 (softcover)
ISBN: 1-4140-3645-0 (hardcover)

This book is printed on acid free paper.

1stBooks – rev. 12/24/03

DEDICATION

To my favorite writers — some of them, sadly, gone — whose many great works have entertained and inspired me:

Isaac Asimov

Lawrence Block

Ray Bradbury

Philip K. Dick

Harlan Ellison

Frederick Exley

Carl Hiaasen

John Irving

Stephen King

Joe R. Lansdale

Dennis Lehane

John D. MacDonald

Barry N. Malzberg

Richard Russo

Robert Silverberg

Kurt Vonnegut

ACKNOWLEDGMENTS

The following stories — many of them in slightly altered form — originally appeared in these magazines:

"A Death Sentence" in *Lime Green Bulldozers,* Number 16 (February 1999).

"The Right Place at the Right Time" in *The Kit-Cat Review,* Volume 1, Number 2 (Autumn 1998).

"Button Eater Bartholomew Pritt on the Bus for the Emotionally Disturbed" in *Enigma,* Winter 2004.

"Bears in the Punch Bowl" in *Words of Wisdom,* Volume 17, Number 3 (December 1997).

"Doodler in Love" in *Enigma,* Winter 2003.

"Garrett Gosch Is Green" in *(000) 000-0000,* published in October 1998 (no issue date or volume number given).

"Suicide Not" in *Mind in Motion,* Winter 1989.

"The Good Parents of Billy Baxter" in *Zeta Magazine,* June 1989.

"Parrot Flop" in *Enigma,* Summer 2003.

"Toys R Fun" in *Enigma,* Spring 2002.

"No One Has Yet Claimed Responsibility for the Bombing" in *Enigma,* Fall 2002.

"Whalewatch" in *Radio Void,* Volume 3, Number 14, 1992.

These stories have not been published previously and appear here for the first time:

"When a Choice Is Not a Choice," "Justice Is Bledsoe's," "Flatus," "Jake Ossinger's Full Life," and "Spray Painting the Side of the Barbershop."

Contents

INTRODUCTION: HOW I CAME TO READ STORIES

Lots of folks, including me, like to read. But it seems most people prefer novels over short stories. A Stephen King fan will be able to tell you all about *Carrie* but not necessarily anything about "The Crate." Some avid readers of novels have even told me they *don't like* reading short stories.

Why this incongruity exists I do not know. In our society of shrinking attention spans and supposedly more bloated personal agendas, I'd think the reading of short stories — because they are *short* and less time-consuming — would fit more perfectly into the daily grind.

For writers, it's harder to get a book of short stories published than it is a novel. So here I come, Mr. Unknown Author, with — what else? — a collection of short stories. Not only that, my next three books will more than likely be short story collections — one in the horror realm, another in the mystery and suspense arenas, and the third in the multifarious universes of fantasy and science fiction. Am I a marketing genius or what? (Now let's not kid ourselves here: I paid 1stBooks to get this baby published, so of course there was no problem there. But I want it to sell, and I know I'm going against the grain, much like a salmon struggling upstream, in trying to attract an audience of readers to what is a collection of short stories.)

I wanted my first book of stories to be what are called *contemporary,* or *mainstream,* works, because I didn't want to be pigeonholed strictly as a horror writer or a mystery writer or any other kind of genre writer. I prefer simply to be regarded as a writer. One of my favorite writers, the late Philip K. Dick, was pigeonholed, if you will, as a science fiction writer. He certainly wrote science fiction, no arguing that, with dozens of sf novels and story collections to his credit, including *Clans of the Alphane Moon, The Man in the High Castle, Solar Lottery, The Preserving Machine,* and *I Hope I Shall Arrive Soon.* But what many casual readers of Dick's science fiction may not know is that, early in his career, he wrote a series of contemporary novels that he was never able to sell The man spent more than twenty years trying to get them published, with no success. That's because he had already been pigeonholed as a science fiction writer. His contemporary books were not published until after his death, when he had a huge and growing cult following. Never mind that these excellent contemporary novels, with such titles as *Mary and the Giant, Humpty Dumpty in Oakland,* and *In Milton Lumky Territory,* were every bit as entertaining as Dick's science fiction. Because his publishers at the time insisted he provide them strictly with sf novels, which supposedly was the only type of fiction his audience would accept from him, the non-sf material remained unpublished for many years.

I enjoy writing science fiction, as well as horror, mysteries, suspense, and fantasies. As a kid, my reading tended toward sf, horror, and fantasy (with the exception of the sword-and-sorcery and Tolkien types, which I have never liked). I discovered the stuff in comic books like *The Fantastic Four, Voyage to the Bottom of the Sea* (also a TV show I never missed), and *The Incredible Hulk.*

(I must digress momentarily to tell an amusing story about my childhood days as a comic book reader. When I was in third grade, I began getting poor marks in school. My parents decided I was spending too much time reading comic books and not enough time studying, so they took my comic books away from me until my grades improved. By this time my older brother, Mike, was a teenager, and our parents felt they could leave the two of us home by ourselves when they went to the store to shop for groceries. If Mike happened to be outdoors doing something and the parents were at the store, I'd go prowling about the house, looking for my confiscated comic books. I searched high and low, in every room of our Millersburg house except one, and I could not find those goddam comic books. The one room I didn't bother checking was my brother's room. My already logical young mind told me my brother hadn't taken away my comic books, so why would they be in his room? But eventually the sneaky part of my logical mind concluded that my parents could have made a deal with Mike to hide the comic books in his room. So one day I decided to search Mike's desk after glancing outside and discovering he was busy playing football with a bunch of friends in our immense back yard. When I opened the big drawer in the lower right-hand corner of Mike's desk, what did I discover? Not my comic books, certainly, but something I quickly decided was even better: a hidden stash of *Playboy* and *Penthouse* magazines. I had never seen anything like these publications! For months after that, whenever I had the opportunity, I'd go into Mike's room, open that desk drawer, and leaf through those marvelous magazines, gazing in fascination at the sexy photos of naked and semi-naked women. *The Incredible Hulk* had never contained anything quite like this! Interestingly enough, I never did find my comic books, nor, from that point on, did I care.)

Eventually I graduated to reading paperback books of science fiction, fantasy, and horror. (Because I couldn't sneak into my brother's room *that* often, I more or less forgot about *Playboy* and *Penthouse* for the time being.) It was upon getting started as a reader of paperbacks that I discovered the sf works of Philip K. Dick. But I get ahead of myself. Let me establish the setting.

For numerous years my family owned a cottage on Lake Wawasee in northern Indiana. We more or less spent entire summers there. Cottage was located just down the road from some fish hatcheries, a bait shop, and a store called Galloway's Groceries. I spent countless mornings and afternoons playing and splashing around in the lake, snorkeling and experiencing a thrill when I'd encounter a fish or a turtle swimming near me. I loved being underwater and, over a long period, conditioned myself to hold my breath for more than two minutes. By late in the day I'd be tired from all the activity, and, with my weekly allowance in hand, I'd walk down to Galloway's Groceries for something to eat or drink, often wearing nothing but my dripping wet swim trunks and a pair of athletic shoes. It was a lake community, and you could walk into stores that way without having to put up with a bitch session from the proprietors about being soaked or shirtless.

Up near the front of Galloway's Groceries were two things that were not food or drink but which immediately captured my attention: a small rack filled with comic books and another small rack containing paperback books. When I say small, I mean *small:* there were only perhaps twenty or thirty comic book titles available at any given time, and as far as the paperback books were concerned, there were maybe thirty or forty different selections, usually with only one copy of each title.

Whenever the family was at our house in Millersburg, comic books were hard for me to buy, because there wasn't a single store in town that sold them (or books or magazines either). I had to travel with my parents in the car to the neighboring town of Goshen, ten miles away, whenever I wanted to get to a store that sold comic books. But here on Lake Wawasee was a very accessible Galloway's Groceries, within walking or bicycling distance of our cottage, where I could go by myself and buy comic books on a weekly, if not daily, basis. (By now my grades in school had improved, and I was permitted to buy comic books again.) I was always more excited than words can describe when a new shipment of *Iron Man* or *Tower of Shadows* or any of my other favorite titles would arrive. Occasionally the new issues would be haphazardly mixed in with old ones that had been there for weeks, and I had to search for them. This I enjoyed; it was like hunting for treasure. Of course, my juvenile brain knew nothing about the distribution side of publishing, so the sudden appearance of these new comic books seemed like a kind of magic to me.

At some point I began to grow curious about that rack of paperback books on its spindle near the comic book rack attached to the front wall of the store. When I'd sort through the comic books, trying to decide which ones my limited funds should go toward, my butt would sometimes bump into the rack of paperbacks directly behind me. So one day, without fanfare, I turned around and began pawing through the paperbacks, studying the covers, the names of the authors, wondering what the books were about and if I should try reading some of them....

I decided to buy an Ace Books edition of *The Game-players of Titan* by some guy named Philip K. Dick. I received no prompting from anyone, and I didn't know a thing about Dick. I think I bought that particular book mainly on the strength of its weird, psychedelic cover. Though today I have no memory of the details of the book's plot — and I never read a book more than once — I do remember racing through it as a kid, enthralled by the story and finding Dick's writing style irresistible. So on future trips to Galloway's Groceries, I purchased other Dick novels as they came in — among them, *Clans of the Alphane Moon* (Ace), *We Can Build You* (DAW), and an Ace "double" featuring *Dr. Futurity* in between the same covers as *The Unteleported Man.*

The next book writer I discovered at Galloway's was the phenomenal Isaac Asimov, who wrote nonfiction as well as fiction — roughly five hundred books altogether, if you can believe it. Within a few years I came to realize this Asimov was a fellow who knew everything about everything and could write clearly and entertainingly about all of it.

When I first saw one of Asimov's books there at Galloway's, however, I was a little put off by his last name, which I wasn't sure how to pronounce. (Remember, I was still a mere ten-year-old.) But one of Asimov's books contained the word "robot" in its title — *I, Robot* (Fawcett), to be specific — and I knew that my comic book hero Iron Man was a robot of sorts. Okay, he was, more accurately, a flesh-and-blood human (Tony Stark) in a high-tech metal suit, but to an undiscerning youngster like me, that was *like* being a robot. So I bought *I, Robot* and read it and liked it every bit as much as the Dick books. I soon bought two more Asimov titles upon discovering them at Galloway's: *Nightfall and Other Stories* and *The Martian Way and Other Stories* (both Fawcett).

Without planning it, I was turning into a science fiction reader. But I think even more important in the formation of my adult reading habits is the fact that, by sheer coincidence, those first three Asimov books were collections of *short stories*. Sure, I really liked reading the Dick novels, but I was also an energetic boy who spent endless hours playing outdoors. Short stories seemed more suited than novels to my routine, because I could read almost any story in one sitting and then go jump in the lake, literally (no pun intended). On the other hand, it took days — often more than a week — to read a single novel.

Before long, at another store, I encountered science fiction magazines. I learned of the existence of sf magazines from trips to the lake town of Syracuse with my mom and my aunt. A drugstore there, the name of which I forget, carried *Analog, Galaxy, Amazing, The Magazine of Fantasy & Science Fiction,* and other digest-size sf periodicals. (This was back when not every drugstore in town seemed like just another branch of a nationwide chain, carrying the same old boring, glossy fashion and lifestyle magazines as every other drugstore, no matter what the branch.) Way up in the top slot of the magazine rack, where I could reach them but was well aware I wasn't supposed to, were *Playboy* and *Penthouse.* But back to the sf magazines.... I noticed some of the authors' names on the contents pages of the magazines were the same as those on the covers of the books at Galloway's Groceries: Philip K. Dick, Isaac Asimov, Frederik Pohl, Poul Anderson.... I was beginning to make connections between different branches of publishing. The magazines fascinated me in a different manner than the books did, and I bought and read plenty of them. In doing so, my reading horizons expanded to writers new to me, like Ray Bradbury and Arthur C. Clarke.

Those horizons continued to grow as the years went by. As a junior high school student, I discovered another writer who made a vast impression on me and whose writing I have followed to the present day: Harlan Ellison, whose "A Boy and His Dog" was anthologized in a pink-colored paperback copy of *World's Best Science Fiction: 1970* (Ace) edited by Donald A. Wollheim and Terry Carr. "A Boy and His Dog" was far different from any previous science fiction story I had read, and I enjoyed it immensely. Also, I encountered a hardback novel by Ray Bradbury, *Something Wicked This Way Comes,* which I read in its entirety in a single afternoon while sitting in the school library. Usually I'm a notoriously slow reader, and the only other book I've ever read in one stint is *The Old Man and the Sea* by Ernest Hemingway.

When summers came to an end and school was about ready to start again, my family would leave the lake behind and head back to our house in Millersburg, where I never entirely forgot about the *Playboy* and *Penthouse* magazines in my brother's room. Probably by accident, I happened to notice that some of the authors whose names were in the science fiction magazines or on the covers of books at Galloway's Groceries — Arthur C. Clarke was one in particular — were also listed occasionally on the contents pages of these adult publications. So I began perusing those magazines not only for their excellent photography but for the chance to read more stories by authors I liked. (Yes, for you stupid people who firmly believe nobody ever opens *Penthouse* or *Playboy* to *read* it, I have now described, with some deliberation, the process by which such an "impossible" reading habit might come about.)

Kent Robinson

After having read thousands of stories by hundreds of writers, I'd have to say I consider Ellison and Bradbury to be the two best short story writers — no matter what the genre — I've ever encountered. They speak to me, as the saying goes. And I'm not exactly limited in my reading. In the thirty-five or so years since I discovered science fiction, I've read all the short stories of John Cheever, and while they were well-written and interesting after a fashion, they were also overly moody and too much like one another. Yes, I've read all the stories of Donald Barthelme, and in spite of the fact that he was widely praised by critics, I never could figure out what the fuck he was writing about. Reading his work was, for me, like going to see some incomprehensible foreign film that the reviewers have unanimously praised, only to find myself sitting there in the theater afterward wondering why. I've read "The Drowned Giant" and "The Waterworks" and "The Mexican Pig Bandit," as well as "Harrison Bergeron" and "The House of Seven Angels" and "Bad Company." I've read Edith Wharton and Stephen Dixon and John Crowley, not to mention Tanith Lee and Robert Bloch and Kate Wilhelm and John Collier. I've read O. Henry and Edgar Allan Poe and Rick Bass and Lorrie Moore and Alice Munro and Ambrose Bierce and William Faulkner and Nathaniel Hawthorne and Ursula K. LeGuin and an army of others. Don't get me wrong: all of these writers have done fine work. I'll even concede that Donald Barthelme wrote superb fiction, and I was just too ignorant to understand it. But I *still* like Ellison and Bradbury most of all.

Here's a list of twenty-five stories I feel are among the best short fiction ever written. My early preoccupation with science fiction and horror have influenced the content of this list. I've included five stories each by Ellison and Bradbury. Some of the stories made their impact on me when I was a mere adolescent; others have impressed me in the not-too-distant past.

Maybe my book of short stories is your first. After you're done reading it, you might want to look for books containing these stories:

1. "A Careful Man Dies" by Ray Bradbury
2. "The Dwarf" by Ray Bradbury
3. "Heavy-set" by Ray Bradbury
4. "The Small Assassin" by Ray Bradbury
5. "A Sound of Thunder" by Ray Bradbury
6. "A Boy and His Dog" by Harlan Ellison
7. "Free with This Box!" by Harlan Ellison
8. "Jeffty Is Five" by Harlan Ellison
9. "The Man Who Was Heavily Into Revenge" by Harlan Ellison
10. "Shatterday" by Harlan Ellison
11. "Nightfall" by Isaac Asimov
12. "In the Hills, the Cities" by Clive Barker
13. "Miss Gentilbelle" by Charles Beaumont
14. "Ridi Bobo" by Robert Devereaux
15. "The Father-thing" by Philip K. Dick
16. "Dolan's Cadillac" by Stephen King
17. "The Graveyard Rats" by Henry Kuttner
18. "Narrow Valley" by R. A. Lafferty
19. "Men under Water" by Ralph Lombreglia
20. "The Colour out of Space" by H. P. Lovecraft
21. "Final War" by Barry N. Malzberg (writing as by "K. M. O'Donnell")
22. "Longtooth" by Edgar Pangborn
23. "Allamagoosa" by Eric Frank Russell
24. "The Thing in the Stone" by Clifford D. Simak
25. "A & P" by John Updike

Since I've mentioned some novels I've read over the years, here's a list of twenty of them that I consider outstanding. You will be struck by how different this list is from the list of short stories in terms of many of the authors whose works are mentioned on it. Once again, though, childhood remains a powerful influence: Philip K. Dick's *The Game-players of Titan* is the first novel I can recall reading, and I rank him as my favorite novelist overall, so I've included five of his magnificent books here.

1. *Clans of the Alphane Moon* by Philip K. Dick
2. *The Game-players of Titan* by Philip K. Dick
3. *Humpty Dumpty in Oakland* by Philip K. Dick
4. *The Man Whose Teeth Were All Exactly Alike* by Philip K. Dick
5. *Puttering About in a Small Land* by Philip K. Dick
6. *A Fan's Notes* by Frederick Exley
7. *The Old Man and the Sea* by Ernest Hemingway
8. *Lucky You* by Carl Hiaasen
9. *The World According to Garp* by John Irving
10. *Desperation* by Stephen King
11. *Mucho Mojo* by Joe R. Lansdale
12. *Among the Missing* by Richard Laymon
13. *To Kill a Mockingbird* by Harper Lee
14. *Gone, Baby, Gone* by Dennis Lehane
15. *Revelations* by Barry N. Malzberg
16. *Empire Falls* by Richard Russo
17. *The World Inside* by Robert Silverberg
18. *The Reproductive System* by John T. Sladek
19. *A Simple Plan* by Scott Smith
20. *Breakfast of Champions* by Kurt Vonnegut

For now, though, we're more concerned with stories, because you're holding a book of them in your hands. A book by *me,* with *my* stories between its covers. Thank you for choosing it. You're the bomb-diggity! I hope you enjoy the read.

Kent Robinson

Like so many of you, the photos from 9/11 that stick in my mind the most are those of innocent people leaping from the World Trade Center to their deaths. Decent Americans were — and should have been — outraged that their fellow citizens were reduced to a fate like this by foreign aggressors. I decided to transform my own indignation into the following story.

WHEN A CHOICE IS NOT A CHOICE

Ernesto glances out the window and sees the airplane as the waiter brings him his usual breakfast: an omelet, a piece of toast (wheat bread always), bacon, orange juice, and coffee. Idly he dismisses the distant plane. He requests a refill on his coffee.

He thinks about his life while he eats. As insurance executives go, he is a remarkably philosophical man. At age forty-seven, he is modestly pleased with his life so far. He has deliberately structured it in certain ways, pursuing specific goals, guiding himself carefully through the years, building on them, like a child patiently assembling a house out of small wooden blocks. Indeed, he thinks as he enjoys his delicious omelet, a life is very much like a house: you can leave one room of a house and enter another, just as you leave one stage of a life to enter another; a house can be filled with love, and so can a life; a house is well-kept or not, and the same is true of a life.

Ernesto does not remember coming to the United States with his parents, because he was only two when the journey occurred. But he knows he made his father proud before he died of the cancer, and his mother, who returned to the city of Morelia after her husband's death to help take care of one of her ailing sisters, is proud of him too. Ernesto sends his mother two hundred dollars each month, but even were she not to receive a dime, she would still love him like a good mother and be proud of what he has accomplished as an American.

"Life is all about choices," his father used to tell him, between cigarette coughs, again and again. "The good ones and the bad ones." It was the choice to smoke that killed him, but he seemed comfortable with the habit up until the very end, and he never expressed any regret over his fatal choice. And to his father's credit, most of the choices the man made in his life were good ones, as far as Ernesto is concerned.

It is a beautiful, cloudless September day in New York City. A brilliant flash of light in the sky barely registers at the edge of Ernesto's field of vision. He looks up from his breakfast on the 106th floor of the North Tower and quickly concludes it was sunlight glinting off the distant plane, which, he thinks nebulously, is less distant now than it was when he first noticed it thirty seconds ago.

Ernesto ponders his tall, beautiful wife, an American woman of French extraction named Lorraine. "Long Lorraine" he sometimes calls her, when surprising her from behind and wrapping his arms around her slim waist or when they are frolicking in bed together, because she is five feet eleven inches tall, with lengthy arms and legs to match her frame and the shimmering downward swoop of her dark blonde hair. He is familiar with many of the things that please her, because, like a decent husband, he makes it his business, his responsibility, to know: picking up after himself around the house; taking her and the children to Yankees games on Saturday afternoons, no matter how much of a slump the team might be in or how interminably Tonya might cry on the way to the stadium; remembering her birthday and their anniversary with modest gifts, like the wristwatch he bought her last November when she turned twenty-nine. He remembers adorning her wrist with the watch after she unwrapped it. She has lovely wrists; he can picture them in his mind, see the tiny, silky hairs sparsely decorating them. Every inch of her is lovely. He loves his lovely wife unconditionally. She was his perfect choice for a mate, and he has never regretted his choice.

And the kids, Tonya, just over a year old, and Rudy, about to turn four. How adorable they are, how innocent. Even when Tonya decides to cry, which is frequently, Ernesto does not get upset, no matter what time of the day or night it is. She's a healthy baby, with healthy lungs most of all; he and Lorraine have had the baby examined often by doctors. All have said she's simply a baby who likes to throw fits, that some babies are that way, that she'll eventually grow out of it, not to worry. So Ernesto frequently finds himself holding the crying Tonya while she wails, and sometimes he giggles as he stares down into the teary-eyed face of his daughter, because she is so cute, even when she is upset. And sometimes, the more he giggles, the louder she cries, and then he giggles even harder, and then she cries harder and louder yet. Lorraine will feign exasperation with the two of them, and she'll remove herself from the room with a look on her face that seems to indicate she suspects her husband and little girl of carrying on some kind of farcical stage routine designed to drive her crazy.

And then there is Rudy, the big baseball fan with the brown eyes and thick head of brown hair. Not yet four, he already grasps certain things about the game, like what a home run and a double play are. When they are at a game, the crack of a Yankees bat signaling that a ball has been hit out near the wall or, better yet, over it, causes Rudy to lurch excitedly in his seat. His eyes spring open to twice their normal size as his gaze tracks the graceful flight of the ball. So cute, thinks Ernesto, sitting next to me in his little Yankees cap and Yankees jersey.

Ernesto loves his two children. He will raise them right, as his parents did him. They will know about responsibility and restraint and the difference between right and wrong. They will learn that real evil exists in the world, as well as good. He and his wife discussed having children before ever getting married, and it was something they both wanted to do. It was their choice, a good choice. They plan to have more.

Ernesto notices it is 8:44 a.m. Almost time to take the elevator down to begin his workday. He looks out the window of the restaurant again, marveling at the endless blue sky. The airplane, he notices with somewhat less obliquity than before, fills more of that sky. A prickling at the back of his neck registers on his consciousness as less than nothing. He sips at his hot cup of coffee, wondering if the service technician will finally show up at his office this morning to fix the huge copier, which has been on the fritz now for two days. Okay, that may have been a bad choice, thinks Ernesto, however small and insignificant it was in the grand scheme of things: the Canon model, though somewhat more expensive, might not have broken down as often as the off brand he ultimately advised his boss to buy.

Managing money is one of the things on which Ernesto prides himself. He tries to save the company money by doing the little things: cutting down on electricity costs by shutting off his computer every night, turning off his lights and those, quite often, of his coworkers. He doesn't try to gouge his clients either, preferring instead to make modest amounts of money off of a greater number of satisfied customers. In terms of his home life, Lorraine is not an extravagant gal, nor does she exhibit the desire to be one — a remarkable quality in a woman, thinks Ernesto. Tonya is too young to understand about money, but Rudy knows not to expect to get every toy he wants. He has been told that everything oosts money and that there is only so much money to spend on those things, so the occasional sacrifice must be made.

Suddenly something inside the restaurant changes in a manner Ernesto has never quite experienced in all the days and months he has eaten breakfast here. His ears register the difference, but he has trouble defining every aspect of it precisely. Not so much an intrusion of new sound as an alteration of the sonority already present: the delicate tinklings of silverware cease; peals of laughter die in merry peoples' throats; no scooting of chairs, less coughing and talking than a moment ago; the restaurant's very air seems to whisper itself into silence as waitresses and busboys halt their brisk movements. Then the tonal quality of those who continue to talk changes: murmured expressions of embryonic alarm replace the buzz of lilting chitchat and idle gossip. Ernesto detects all of this, however indistinctly, in a mere second or two. He places his empty cup back on its saucer with an almost undetectable porcelain click and surveys the other patrons. Seventy, maybe eighty people. Everyone seems to be mumbling warily about the same thing, whatever it is. Then he notices the heads, lowered ever so slightly between shoulders and turned, when necessary, in the direction of the windows. A couple of women looking over, rather than at, the open compacts they are holding in front of them. Unblinking eyes frozen and glazed as almost everybody focuses their attention outside the windows.

Ernesto, with the poor peripheral vision, again turns his head and looks out the window next to him for a third or fourth time. The airplane, a Boeing 767, is quite large in the sky now, a disorienting visual violation of the blue, and it is flying directly toward their building. It is sleek and shiny, moving fast, and Ernesto knows the craft is not about to divert its course and miss them at the last instant. Beads of sweat form on his upper lip, his neck, his back. He clutches the edges of his small table, every muscle in his body tensing. That plane, he thinks, having difficulty processing the information, is really going to hit this tower.

The plane smacks into the side of the two-hundred-foot-wide structure an indeterminate number of floors below the two that the restaurant occupies. Ernesto turns his eyes away at the last second; there is something too horrifying, too unnatural, in watching the massive craft rushing through the air a few hundred feet beneath him rather than miles overhead, where flying machines belong in a rational world. The Boeing changes from an inanimate product of technology to a living, bloodthirsty monster on the attack. Upon impact the whole restaurant shudders, people scream, a handful of tables and chairs tip over, framed paintings fall off the walls, and a series of popping sounds, like fireworks, ensues. A waitress drops her tray as she struggles for balance. A sprinkling system line bursts open and begins hissing out water in a far corner. Pots and pans tumble and clang, unseen, in the kitchen. A loud pop close to Ernesto causes him to jump backward out of his seat as the window nearest him cracks down the center, becoming a pair of jagged pieces of glass that fall out of their frame completely, dropping toward the street below. He feels the air sucking at him, beckoning him out into the open sky, like an invisible demon tempting him to make a bad choice, but its influence is weak, and he is far enough away from the open rectangle to resist its pull.

Steel groans within the guts of the tower. The sound is among the most terrible Ernesto has ever heard, worse even than the shrill cries of his fellow diners: strong metal girders underneath him adjusting to the enormous weight they support after being bent in abnormal ways that no longer allow for such ponderousness. A muffled explosion occurs, sounding like a distant giant grumbling to wakefulness, then another, then a third that spits swirling balls of flame out into the sky, this last eruption causing the restaurant to vibrate. While the lights flicker, some older people stagger about, and in a moment that strikes Ernesto as perversely comic, they appear to be dancing at a club featuring a poor excuse for strobe lighting. When the noises from below briefly recede, a plate can be heard spinning crazily, as if providing weird background music for the "dancers," as well as for the human choir of sobs and coughs and gasps of disbelief.

Then: nothing.

The protests of the steel taper off, restaurant glass no longer shatters, the crash of decor ends. The patrons — most of whom are standing at their tables, still as statues, a few others who are helping their friends or loved ones up off the floor

— have suffered a jolt but seem to be recovering with remarkable rapidity. A handful are pulling cell phones out of their pockets or purses to make calls. Ernesto remembers leaving his phone in his office the previous afternoon. He notes the resumption of his own breathing but is unaware of when he stopped exhaling. Gusts of wind blow in through the restaurant's broken windows, causing napkins to flutter. Ernesto watches a group of men nervously toss some bills onto their table and leave the establishment.

The near calm does not last long. Even as Ernesto regains his composure sufficiently to begin considering his own departure, another explosion takes place below him in the belly of the building. He witnesses something he is totally unprepared for: an entire section of flooring gives way, falling through to some lower region, and Ernesto happens to be looking at the area in question as he sees perhaps thirty people drop out of sight, many of them screaming and waving their hands above them as they plummet downward.

That didn't just happen, he thinks. My God, all those people.... This can't be happening. Yet he is a rational man who trusts the input of his senses, and he realizes that the terrible events unfolding around him are indeed happening.

Ernesto wishes he had remembered his cell phone. He wants to call Lorraine. He wants to tell her how much he loves her, because he has told her this only a few thousand times, and his heart always reminds him that one more time will not be too many.

The four men who left the restaurant minutes ago return, looking shaken, their suits sprinkled with plaster dust. Three of them are further rattled to see part of the floor, and many of the diners, missing. As a kind of cruel public service announcement, the fourth man says loudly, so that everyone in the establishment can hear him, that the elevators are not working and too much smoke fills the stairwells to negotiate them. As if confirming this last, Ernesto begins to smell smoke.

He believes he is going to die. He wants to take Rudy to one more Yankees game before that occurs, to gently tap an index finger on Tonya's adorable button nose as she insists on wailing for no reason whatsoever, to kiss his wife's neck and cheeks and lips, but above and beyond and through all of those earnest attempts to distract himself — those yearnings for one more chance to experience glorious life — wafts the cold realization that he is going to die very soon. They are trapped at the top of this tall tower, and no way will firefighters be able to rescue them in time.

He has never thought about death a lot, but then, who would, given his circumstances? He has always experienced good health, as have his wife and children, and death has never seemed to be anything but an inevitable reality lurking unthreateningly on some dark, distant horizon. Now death has come calling, has crept far too close, the horizons narrowing, on this deceptively sunny day.

On hands and knees, someone has crawled over close to the opening left by the collapsed floor and is peering down into the hole. His jaw drops. "They're — too far — they — God, they must be dead!" he shrieks. "I see fire!" Ernesto doesn't need to risk taking a look for himself to know that several floors below the one on which he stands have probably given way too.

Now smoke is visible as it rises up into the restaurant from below. Ernesto doesn't see it until after an elderly woman with glasses tugs at his outstretched arm and repeatedly asks him if he is all right. He blinks, looks at her, then slowly lowers his arm. He licks his lips and blinks some more, partly against the smoke and partly to bring his mind back to reality. The woman continues to pull at his arm, inquiring as to whether he is okay. During this crisis, when self-preservation should automatically be a priority, a kind stranger has demonstrated a concern for another individual, for him. He looks at the woman as she takes a step backward, and nods, indicating he is fine. Almost immediately, as if in contradiction to that nod, he coughs hard upon inhaling some smoke that drifts past him. Doubled over, he checks his watch as the coughing subsides. It is 9:32. Impossible, he thinks. How long have I been standing here with my arm extended, my mind adrift? It seems like the plane struck only minutes ago, but almost an hour has passed. What have I been doing? Am I in shock? He doesn't know if you can wonder if you're in shock while actually in that state, but clearly it doesn't matter. Only survival matters. He decides he will keep the old lady near him, in case he has to help her as she has helped him, but he notices she has wandered off. Thicker smoke pours into the restaurant from the hole in the floor. Numerous people can be heard, if not seen, coughing in the swirling grayness. Lumps appear in the carpet near Ernesto's feet as heat from the conflagration below causes the floor to bubble.

The outer steel tubes that provide support for the building are groaning again, louder than ever, as heat from the fire weakens them and they are increasingly unable to support the weight they carry. The sound makes Ernesto want to scream. Maybe he does scream. He isn't sure. Tears fill his eyes, a response to the smoke and to his feelings of sorrow, of outrage. How can a life — *his* life — end like this? No one is coming for them, no one can, and he is going to die. They are all going to die.

Screaming. There is screaming, he is not imagining it. Is it the steel? The sound of the straining metal is awful, unearthly, like a death knell. But no, it is something else. Some*one*. Him? Not him. He can hardly breathe, let alone scream. His heart races madly. The screams are coming from more than one throat, from over by the broken windows. They are loud at first, then dwindle away, only to be replaced by more loud cries. Ernesto squints through the smoke in the direction of the windows.

People are jumping out of them. Screaming on the way down.

They have made a choice. Tips of flame are starting to poke up through isolated sections of the floor, and Ernesto knows it is only a matter of minutes, maybe seconds, until they all burn to death or die of asphyxiation. He cannot imagine death by smoke or fire. Sweat pours down his face. What should he do? He must make a choice. What kind of options does he have? Confronting him are only a bad choice — jump to his death — or a worse choice — die by fire.

He clenches his fists and presses them against the sides of his skull. The fire is close, the floor is weakening. He staggers, he is out of air to breathe. But there is air out there, the beautiful blue sky is filled with it. He has to breathe, he can't wait to die by fire, the heat is already unbearable, to die like that would take too long, be too agonizing.

Ernesto stumbles over to a broken window and centers himself in its frame, then backs up several yards before racing toward it and leaping out of the tower. He has made a choice. He closes his eyes tightly and will not open them again. He does not want to see the ghastly sight of the huge, uncaring building next to him that betrayed him in the end, that wanted to be his tomb. He cannot bear to take in the equally dreadful vision of the great distance he is plunging, of the planet that is pulling him down to kill him. He refuses to see, to think, to feel. It is hard, he is scared, he hopes he dies of a heart attack before he hits. He does not scream on the way down, he will not give death the satisfaction. That is his final choice.

Suicide is illegal, but should it be? I don't have a strong opinion on the subject one way or the other, but if pressed on it, I'd probably opt for freedom and say no. I just wish those who screw up when attempting to off themselves would get it right more often, thereby saving hospital emergency room personnel lots of needless headaches.

The character who narrates the following story definitely has an opinion on whether he ought to be able to commit suicide, but his circumstances are a great deal different than those of most of us.

"A Death Sentence," in its title and increasingly frantic tone, is a bit of a homage to the excellent Dorothy Parker short story "A Telephone Call."

A DEATH SENTENCE

Leave me be. Why bother to save me? What the hell is the point? I am beyond salvation, the state has indicated as much by its sentence, yet now you try to perform this rescue operation. Why? Why? So that you can punish me further, so that you yourselves can — imagine it — kill me.

Go ahead, look at each other and ask yourselves who gave him the sedatives, where did he get them. You'll never figure it out, and I'll never tell. I am, quite frankly, past all telling at this point. Dozens of people are in and out of the prison infirmary each day. All of them sneaked me sedatives. None of them did. Other inmates. Guards. No, wait, I forgot, the pills didn't come from the infirmary; visitors brought them. You scratch your heads and attempt to piece it together, assholes. What do I care what conclusions you reach? One way or the other, I will be dead by midnight. Just so I die by my own hand. Let go of my arm. Leave me be.

I'm not eager to die, you know. It's silly to want to die before you've had a chance to grow tired of life. Old people, incurably sick people — their desire to end it all I can understand. But here I am, compelled to commit suicide as a reasonably healthy thirty-five-year-old man. Better I take my own life than let the state take it. A final act of dignity, of freedom, on my part seems essential. Suicide as dignified: there's one for you.

If I could speak over the drug, I would tell you your efforts are futile. Go away, I would say, take a coffee break, look the other way for a few minutes, leave me be, what do you care. I swallowed the pills, a billowing handful of them, a good thirty minutes ago, so it shouldn't be long until the final curtain closes, no, it shouldn't be long now. And it's no skin off your butts. You are just lackeys of the state. You are just doing your job. By the way, doesn't it make you feel ashamed when you are forced into a position where you must admit you are just doing your job? And doesn't the saying of it make you not want to do it? And, furthermore, since you can easily make such a shameful admission, it seems to me that you could just as easily do the added shameful thing and not do your job. But I suppose that would require some backbone, some thread of character, a noble resistance to authority. And we all know where that kind of behavior gets you, now don't we?

If I could speak, I would tell you you're too late, there's no way you'll be able to pump my stomach in time, so just forget it, just go away. Fuck you, fuck the guard, fuck every guard in this place, and that greasy, sleazy warden too. Already I note the sleepiness, the lethargy in my limbs, the unexpected and frankly bizarre, though certainly not unwelcome, telescoping vision, and of course the loss of speech control. I am not a stupid man, I did not wind up here because I am stupid, I know what I've done and how wonderful it felt and what will happen as a result. I am attempting to end this hopeless series of events known as my life with a little dignity. I'll bet if I started counting to five hundred by fives, I'd be dead before I was done.

Go away. Leave me alone. Get your fucking hands off my arms!

A flower. That is what I see when thirteen-year-old Amanda Hunter's delicate, freckled face blossoms in my memory. She was not the only one, mind you, but merely the latest, the one who landed me in this hellhole. Amanda, a showy, teasing lily, like all of them, unscented but spectacular to view, eager to be plucked, to possess fragrance. And so I plucked her! Brought her to full bloom! Gave the lily redolence where none should be! is that a crime? Well, yes, apparently so, though I don't know why, don't understand it one bit, no, I'm not just being stubborn, let me be clear in saying it's not as if this were some totally innocent child, though I suppose whether she deserved, ultimately, to be murdered is a fair subject for argument, could be debated for decades in fact, or maybe not, what do I know, locked in here for so long. I know of the outside world only what my lawyer — a loopy, feckless sort of man who hates his job and his existence — chooses to tell me, and even then it's not necessarily the case that I listen, so tired am I of seeing the slimy twerp, given what little he's done for me.

Five hundred. Five hundred by fives. I don't know why you're bothering to strap me onto this stretcher, to go to all this frantic effort, because surely before I am even able to count to five hundred by fives, I will be dead. Haven't I told you this already? Haven't I pleaded with you to leave me alone, to leave me be? Let a human being, or even someone you may regard as a thing significantly less than a human being but nevertheless still a man, mark off his final minutes harmlessly and as he sees fit. Five hundred by fives. You sons of bitches won't even get me as far as the ambulance parked outside, let alone to the hospital across town. Who do you think you are? Leave me alone, I just want to be left alone, to surrender to sensory shutdown as the pills take effect. It's happening already, it's in the late or at the very least late middle stages, there's no turning back, no helping me. You fools, you stupid, stupid fools. It's either the pills now or the lethal injection later, and after all, after all, what difference does it make to you?

Little Amanda Hunter, squeaking and flailing as I lugged her off into the shadowy, damp depths of the woods, where I plucked her petals, committed my crime as determined by the state, pummeling, slashing. Deep down she wanted it, she begged for it. She called to me through her screams, no meant yes, the message shot out of her wide eyes and into my gut, activating my muscles, the trees and loam and nearby stream acting as a chorus, urging me to go through with the killing, assisting me actually, it was a natural act, a thing in and of nature. Her big, frightened eyes reflected shards of moonlight there in the darkness, beneath the leafy, conspiratorial limbs, atop the soft ground that functioned as accessory, the running water whispering, *Yes, proceed, finish her off, pluck the lily.* So I took the ax and, well, you know the rest, no need to go into ridiculously graphic detail here, I really *did* pluck her, if you see what I mean, separating limbs from torso like all the times before, flinging these particular arms and legs into the beckoning stream, doing my lunar dance as her blood spilled over me, getting careless, forgetting to wear gloves, my prints winding up everywhere. No, no, I am not insane, that useless flunky the court appointed for me keeps wanting to use that defense, but I won't allow it, I've told him no, forget it, nature talks to me, it talks to all of us, we are a part of nature and nature a part of us. How simple, how basic, is this equation? Nothing crazy about it.

If I could live I would live, but the state has determined that I can't, so I will take charge here. Screw the death penalty, and screw those idiots outside holding candles in protest of it. This isn't a political thing, you must understand, not political at all. We're talking personal here, a final, feeble thrust in the direction of dignity.

Dow the hall we go. Clatter, clatter, hey, what's the matter? I hope the wheels get jammed up. That occurs all the time with shopping carts in grocery stores.

Why not now? I hope you both fall down and sprain your knees. Or die of fucking heart attacks. No, now that I think about it, I don't wish those things, because there's simply not enough time left, and therefore I have nothing against you two, you seem like nice fellows, all things considered. Just doing your jobs, just doing your jobs. One fluorescent light flying by overhead, two, three.... Not many lights left, boys, I'm telling you. And so very far away they are. Clickety-clack, clickety-clack, down the hall we go, rolling, rolling, rolling, keep this deathbed rolling.... Those lights are getting dimmer by the second. We're just around the corner from the prison exit and, frankly and wonderfully, a somewhat more dramatic exit. Thank you for wasting your time and mine. Certainly there is irony here: save me so I can be executed. Tell the warden he's a bastard. Fuck him. Though we move, we get nowhere. I am going to die tonight, and I'll do it my way.

Five hundred by five, you pricks. Five, ten, fifteen, twenty, twenty-five, thirty, thirty-five, forty....

Kent Robinson

When I lived in southern California, I was an extra in several films, including Assassination, *mentioned in the following story. The details of a typical day on a movie set were just like I describe them here. As with all of my stories, however, please don't read too much into this one: none of the characters are real, merely products of my imagination.*

THE RIGHT PLACE AT THE RIGHT TIME

Had I been a movie reviewer, I'd have labeled Charles Bronson's *Assassination* a "bad film." That the widely unanticipated sequel, *Assassination 2,* was apparently in production validated the old truism: if bad films made money, they were followed by bad sequels (or, in all fairness to the unfinished *Assassination 2,* a sequel that would more than likely be bad).

But I wasn't a movie reviewer. I wasn't a writer of any sort. I was an actor. Well, okay, an extra. By joining enough nickel-and-dime agencies, I was able to work maybe three weeks per month. At fifty to a hundred bucks a day, cash, I did all right, even though there were no benefits, and you never had a feeling of job security no matter how steadily the roles, so-called, poured in. Gone was the protective embrace of the National Education Association that I'd been used to.

I was a reporter in *Assassination.* Twelve hours in Marina del Rey shooting a scene that lasted five minutes in the movie. I'm visible in the lower right-hand corner of the screen. I sat in front of the little weasel who stood up during the press conference and asked the First Lady — played by the late Jill Ireland — a bunch of hostile questions pertaining to her black eye. In 1987, the year *Assassination* was made, I easily could have won the Academy Award for best head turn by an extra, had such a category existed.

29

Bronson wasn't returning for the sequel (what did that tell you?), but my skill as an extra had been so awe-inspiring that the studio was dying to get me back. Yeah, right. Actually some sniveling assistant to an assistant had no doubt dialed the first phone number that came to mind — in this case, that of Christie Hutchins Enterprises — and barked, "Get us some extras!" I was listed with Christie's company, as well as Extras Special, which had landed me the original *Assassination* gig, so the fact that I got called for both projects was pure coincidence.

"I can't believe they're making a sequel to that piece of shit," I told Christie over the phone. As a reviewer, I would have dubbed *Assassination* "bad" only because newspapers wouldn't have allowed me to use the phrase "piece of shit."

"You saw the first one?" Christie asked.

"I was <u>in</u> the first one." I was grumpy, with hangover. It was early Sunday morning, and she'd awakened me. "When's the last time you pulled my resumé and looked at it? I update the damned thing with you people four times a year. Would it interest you to learn I just finished making *Ax Hacker?* Do you care? If you'd cultivate your clients more thoroughly, maybe we'd get speaking parts once in a — "

"Johnny," she said, "I don't want to hear this at four in the morning. We provide extras; that's our function. It's up to you to find your own speaking parts. Go to CAA. I've got two thousand resumés on file. Exactly how much time do you think I have to sit around staring at yours? In any event, I'm not at the office; I'm at home in bed with my trusty Rolodex and a book of phone numbers. Seventy-five extras are required for *Assassination 2* by eight o'clock. It's going to take me three hours just to make the necessary calls. Then maybe I'll be able to eat breakfast or go to the bathroom. Probably not, however, because by then somebody *else* will call wanting *more* extras five minutes ago. By the way, congratulations on *Ax Hacker.* Who got you that?"

"Big Name Extras."

"Oh, Big Name! That's good."

Christie told me that, other than making sure I had on dark shoes, I could wear pretty much what I wanted to the *Assassination 2* set, because wardrobe would be handing out black jumpsuits. We'd be on the roof of a tall building in downtown Los Angeles, posing as a squad of martial arts fighters in training.

I hung up, dragged myself out of bed, and ate my usual unhealthful breakfast of bacon and sugar-coated cereal. After a long, steamy shower, I brushed my teeth, threw on a T-shirt and some shorts, and read the morning newspaper until it was time to leave. By seven-thirty I was heading south on the Pasadena Freeway, my hangover having pretty much dissolved into a dull awareness that, whether I liked it or not, a new day had dawned.

I found myself in an introspective mood, reflecting upon my ten years as an extra. I'd given up teaching high schoolers to pursue acting. At this point I couldn't honestly remember why. The challenge? The search for something different? Undue influence from the memory of a college girlfriend who told me I'd make a great actor after she saw me in a campus production of *Bus Stop?* So would Hollywood *ever* offer me a meaty role, complete with dialogue or at least some closeup facial expressions, that would put me on the road to stardom? I felt silly merely asking myself the question. The odds were astronomically against me. I knew it; every extra did. Lifelong anonymity was a potential fate that, for the well-being of our egos, we were better off not pondering. But because of my Midwestern upbringing, my feet were firmly rooted on the ground, so I couldn't help thinking about the harsher realities from time to time.

I parked my VW on a crummy side street and tried three pairs of glass doors before coming upon the unlocked set that led into the building where we'd be filming. The place was cold, dark, and — down here anyway — utterly abandoned,

31

lacking even a security guard. I managed to locate the elevators and rode one to the top floor, as Christie had instructed me to do. From there, she had said, a short flight of stairs opened out onto the roof.

When the elevator doors parted, the sights and sounds of a movie set assaulted my senses: an obese man checking in extras and yelling very loudly and angrily whenever he had to repeat himself; the rustling of costumes; tables and chairs being moved, then moved back to their original locations minutes later by others; the laughter of predominantly female crew members whose outbursts were not genuine expressions of mirth but rather a loud way of maintaining sanity in such a hectic, stressful environment; Styrofoam cups being crushed after all the coffee in them had been drank....

Approximately fifty extras, both male and female, were squirming into or adjusting their jumpsuits. I got in line behind three guys at a table with a hastily scrawled EXTRAS sign taped to the front. Soon I was talking to the fat dude.

"Johnny Greene, Christie Hutchins Enterprises."

"You're late," he said, flipping through some papers.

He was wrong. I'd been told I was late countless times by these cloddish attendance takers who invariably reminded me of aging bikers; it was just something they always said to me. Something about my personal appearance or the sound of my voice, I figured. Fatso hadn't made any such remark to the trio ahead of me.

It was ten till eight. I was sick and tired of always being told I was late.

"I'm not late. Christie said to be here at — "

" — seven-thirty."

"No she didn't; she said eight o'clock."

"You were supposed to be here at seven-thirty." Fatso gestured to another table, behind which were two gaudy women and several racks of jumpsuits. "They'll get you an outfit," he said, having already put our verbal exchange behind him.

I was handed a nylon jumpsuit and promptly stepped into it and zipped it up around me. My car radio had informed me the temperature would hit a hundred degrees today. By noon I'd be roasting inside this outfit.

More extras were trickling in off the elevators as I ascended the stairs to the roof. Cameras, lights, and microphones were positioned everywhere, with thick, black electrical cables curling among them. Crew members, pawing the walkie-talkies at their belts, scurried from one ugly piece of technology to another, appearing more disorganized than busy. Some extras had stretched themselves out over the four-foot-high cement wall that enclosed the roof, their bottoms twitching with apprehension as they peered down at Wilshire Boulevard some thirty stories below. I heard the word "vertigo" bandied about more times than I cared to count. Nobody used the term "dizziness." One person had said "vertigo," so they all said "vertigo," like sheep. Maybe it was because extras were movie buffs, and Alfred Hitchcock, one of the household names, had made a film called *Vertigo.* Or did the repeated use of the word "vertigo" reveal a sad truth about us extras — that our impulse was to follow, not lead, which made us natural candidates for providing background for the DeNiros and Streeps, never to become luminaries ourselves?

From behind I recognized the diminutive figure and medium-length black hair of Margie, another extra. We'd met two years ago while working on Zuma Beach Bloodsuckers. She had looked too fine in a bikini. It had turned out that, like me, she enjoyed reading science fiction and watching the Three Stooges. For six months we'd gone out pretty regularly, but then, for one of those vague, unspoken reasons that neither party is willing to explore, we'd stopped calling each other. It had been almost a year since our paths had crossed.

"Is that who I think it is?" I asked as I sidled up to her at the wall.

Margie looked over her shoulder at me. "Johnny!" she exclaimed, turning

33

around so we could hug each other. I kissed her on the cheek and then joined her and the rest of the extras in gazing down at Wilshire.

"Quite a drop, huh?"

I nodded. "Does it make you dizzy?"

She laughed as if she understood my irritation over having heard the word "vertigo" once too often.

"So how you been?"

She flashed me an arctic smile that indicated she found my inquiry insincere. "I thought maybe you'd left L. A.," she said.

"Why would you think that?"

She shrugged. "So many people are. My friend Pam — you remember her? — she moved back to Nebraska just last week. I'm planning to visit her at Christmastime."

"Yeah, I remember Pam. Tell her I said hi."

"People are leaving in other ways too. This married couple I knew since my college days — they both died of AIDS complications. *Both* of them! They went so quickly. Some folks hang on for ages, but others.... He got it from some prostitute and passed it on to his wife. The prostitute is still alive and kicking, last I heard."

"Was that Eric and Meredith?"

"Yes, Eric and — yes, that's right, you *did* meet them, just before — " Abruptly she fell silent, but the words she hadn't spoken were loudest of all.

"Just before I quit calling you," I said.

A woman with a brush and a spray can was moving from extra to extra, combing their hair. Warm gusts of wind made her efforts difficult.

"You know," I said, "it's funny. I've never personally known anyone with AIDS."

Margie squinted at me in anger and confusion. "Exactly what is that supposed to mean, Johnny? Why is that funny?"

"Well I didn't mean *funny* funny — "

"You say that so smugly, as if it's a medal you wear."

"Jesus, Margie, take it — "

"And why *didn't* you call?" Her eyes were suddenly moist with tears. "What did I do? What *didn't* I do?"

I held out my arms, and after some hesitation, she let me hug her again. "It wasn't you," I explained. "It was me. It's always been me."

She pulled away from me, more confused than ever. "What are you talking about?"

"I don't *know* what I'm talking about." It was my turn to be upset. "It's just — it's some kind of personality defect. I'm an intelligent person, but sometimes I simply do things — or stop doing them — without regard for the consequences. I never start anything that way; I try to think it through ahead of time. But I always think it won't matter when I stop something. Maybe I have a heightened sense of being trapped, which is why I quit jobs or leave women so abruptly. I don't know."

"Well," said Margie with a feeble smile, "in order to stop with me, did you start a relationship with somebody else?"

I shook my head no.

At that point the lady combing the extras' hair reached Margie and me and made us look pretty.

Moments later a guy who looked like Cat Stevens on speed approached our group and yelled into a bullhorn. "Extras, listen up!"

Everyone quickly quieted down. The only noises were made by the wind and a distant helicopter.

"My name is Dave," the guy with the bullhorn continued, "and I'm the assistant director for this movie, which is called *Assassination 2*. I take my orders from the director, and all of you take your orders from me."

Seasoned extras like Margie and me had heard this standard intro a million times. The only things that ever changed were the names of the people and the movies. Next Dave would stress how important we extras were."

"I want to emphasize," he said, "that just because you're extras, it doesn't mean you're not important."

This of course meant that in certain ways having to do with money, stardom, and ego, we *weren't* that important. Stallone and Eastwood never had to be reminded by some flunky that they were important.

The helicopter was getting closer, judging by the increasingly loud whir of its rotor blades as they sliced through the atmosphere. Dave's comments were still readily discernible, but I lost track of what he was saying as my mind fogged over with thoughts of Margie. Memories of our time together. Did she want to get back together? Was she currently unattached? Many people believed that success — in relationships, in jobs — depended on being in the right place at the right time, as if the entirety of someone's destiny hinged on being at that one right place at that one right time. I found that to be a terribly despairing philosophy. I liked to think that fate wasn't so cruel as to deny us a second chance once in a while.

The helicopter was so loud now that I feared it was about to descend upon us. Dave, unable to compete with the flying machine's noise, lowered his bullhorn. All of us looked up at the sky in every direction, but no chopper could be seen. Then one of the extras ran to the wall, glanced down over the side of the building, and waved to the rest of us. Like a flock of seagulls we swarmed over to the wall, peering over it just in time to see the helicopter flying beneath the level of our roof, between our building and the one across the wide street below.

"Cool!" someone hollered.

The chopper, like a gigantic insect, floated past in what appeared to be slow motion. It was so close I was foolishly tempted to lower my hand and try to touch it, as if it were a child's toy. When it was directly beneath me, I imagined myself leaping onto it, my whole being magically gliding unharmed through the deadly blades and metal engine cowl that separated me from the cockpit, and flying to someplace far away. A few seconds later the helicopter was gone, nothing but a shrinking black bug on the horizon.

Responding to the commands of the assistant director, we extras arranged ourselves in five rows of fifteen people each. One of the movie's supporting actors would be leading us in stretching, thrusting, and bending exercises — ninja drills, in other words.

For what seemed like an eternity, Dave quietly conferred with one of his coworkers. Everything on a movie set took far longer than it should have.

"All right," he finally said into his bullhorn, "the script calls for one of you to yell out. Your line is, 'Come on, you idiots, let's get serious!'"

Here was a rarity: I'd worked on a lot of projects, and seldom did an extra get to deliver a line. Maybe once every fifty films. Today some extra was going to make a minimum of a thousand dollars instead of a maximum of a hundred, all because he or she would get to speak. That person would subsequently be able to join the actors' union, after which powerful organizations like the Creative Artists Agency might very well offer representation. The hand beckoning toward fame and fortune would at least reach out halfway.

Dave was pointing a finger in my direction. "You — "

Was he indicating me? Was I at the right place at the right time? Was I finally going to get my first big chance?

"You," Dave said again. "The girl — the woman with the dark hair. Give it a shot."

It was Margie.

She giggled and shouted, "Come on, you idiots, let's get serious!"

"Lose the giggle, and do it louder," said Dave.

"Come on, you idiots, let's get serious!"

"Good." Another long pause while Dave talked some more with a different co-worker than before. Then he looked up and said to Margie, via the bullhorn, "Before you leave today, make sure you see me. You'll have to sign some papers."

With her single line, Margie had set significant wheels in motion. Now she was going to get to sign special papers. She was still serving Dave, but six months or a year from now, on a different movie, maybe she'd have a supporting role, and maybe Dave would be serving her. Coddling her, keeping her happy. The papers she would sign were documents necessary for her to receive her heightened pay. She wouldn't have to stand in line for thirty minutes to get a wad of dirty cash from a fat creep who was incapable of civility. Later today perhaps Dave would ask her to dinner, an offer she wouldn't refuse, because at dinner he might ask her to audition for a speaking part in a TV miniseries he'd be directing after *Assassination 2.*

I mumbled the words to myself. *Come on, you idiots, let's get serious!* I could have said them better than Margie had. It wasn't fair. I was happy for Margie — a little bit anyway — but what about my big chance? What about being in the right place at the right time? Did I have to slave away anonymously on another fifty or sixty movie sets before seven new words came along? Or three? Or even one?

I decided I'd had my fill of being an extra. But what would I do? I had stopped teaching, and I didn't want to go back to it. I'd stopped seeing Margie, and I didn't want to resume that part of my life either. I seldom went back to anything. I didn't know what I wanted in the foreseeable future, but I realized that, true to form, I was experiencing an overwhelming need to stop doing something.

So I'd stop being an extra. No more so-called acting. Today was it; *Assassination 2* would be my final film. How pathetic.

I squinted off into the distant sky, searching for the helicopter that had flown by a while ago. But it had disappeared. I wondered where it was going.

Kent Robinson

I have little to say about this story, other than I think it has a certain warped charm to it. I wrote it years ago — clear back in the 1980s — so the terrorist element is not a prose development evolving from the 9/11 incidents.

BUTTON EATER BARTHOLOMEW PRITT ON THE BUS FOR THE EMOTIONALLY DISTURBED

Bartholomew Pritt — we sometimes call him "Button Eater," but affectionately so — became a hero of sorts, in one of those rare ways that is possible only for someone who is emotionally disturbed.

In achieving his heroic stature, Button Eater lost his left earlobe, and the longest of the five bones in the metatarsus of my right foot was shattered.

Ours is a rather large school district compared to most others in the state, so we have an ample amount of emotionally disturbed students who ride a bus to a special institute five days a week. I'm Dr. Bernard Rosenthal — the kids call me "Bernie," also affectionately so — and I, too, ride the bus for the emotionally disturbed. I am the school district's psychologist, trained in emotional disorders, child psychology, idiolalia, infantile perversion, and Freudianism.

I ride the bus to keep tabs on the kids and help make sure they behave. Ed, the driver, can't do everything; his job of making sure our ten-year-old clunker of a bus makes the trip to the institute and back each day without breaking down is tough enough.

Supervising the kids is necessary, because sometimes things can really get out of hand on the bus for the emotionally disturbed. Like the time Justin Mendoza attacked Ritchie Brillstein with a potted cactus. School administrators had trouble hiring someone to serve as a bus monitor for one hour a day, so I agreed to let them

41

make riding the vehicle one of my job duties when they renegotiated my contract last year.

Every weekday morning the parents drop off their emotionally disturbed children at the high school most centrally located within the district. The kids climb on board the bus, and off we go to the institute, returning late each afternoon to waiting moms and dads.

On the day that Button Eater became a hero, his love for Sharon Fegley was, at long last, reciprocated; that, for Button Eater, was the most cherished consequence of his heroic deed. The praiseful feature articles on him in all four local papers were nice, as was his chance to ride with the grand marshal in the following year's Memorial Day parade. But all true heroes eventually need to acquire the romantic partners of their dreams, and Button Eater certainly got his.

A group response to Button Eater's actions occurred that — because it involved nearly our entire busload of terrific youngsters — outshone even the love that blossomed between Bart and Sharon. After Button Eater performed his heroic deed, the kids thanked him and hugged him and so forth — normal behavior, by customary standards.

In other words, maybe my emotionally disturbed group isn't as weird as some people in the community think. After all, the students reacted properly after Button Eater made their lives safe again.

Furthermore, maybe some of those judgmental community folks are more maladjusted than they care to admit. Like Carl Spacklin, a former fast-food employee who one day fancied himself a Haganah terrorist.

If nothing else, Button Eater's rise to fame reaffirms my belief that everybody has a place somewhere in the world. Even those who eat buttons or fondle themselves in public, for instance.

Nine-year-old Bartholomew's habit of devouring buttons is not a disease in and of itself, obviously, but rather the most noticeable symptom of the situation neurosis from which he suffers. For some reason, he becomes violent when he sees buttons on people's clothing. Upon spotting a button, he charges at it like a starving man lunging for food. As a result, he has ruined countless items of apparel and cost his poor mother hundreds of dollars.

In his assault on buttons, Bart is not choosy about his victims: he has pounced on a policeman, a grandmother, and even a priest, almost choking the last person to death in an effort to consume the black button located near his shiny white collar. Although Bart is only a child, his strength is phenomenal when he enters one of his neurotic rages.

He's one of the half dozen or so kids on our bus whom I classify as an extreme case. We also have the usual crop of bed wetters who are too old and escapist children with strangely skewed ideas of reality.

The fact that all of us on the bus have learned to ride with one another without too many problems is an accomplishment more uplifting than I can describe. The world outside the bus is full of communities where most people get along fairly well, but the kids and I have our own harmonious community. After several months of encouraging the students to accept, and interact with, one another, I feel quite comfortable on board the bus. I'm proud of the kids and my successes with them. The bus can be a rather cozy environment, in its own way, and it's definitely more relaxed than the institute, where certain members of our group sometimes get uptight about having to mingle with emotionally disturbed youths from other school corporations.

Twelve-year-old Sharon Fegley, Bart's object of desire, is terribly withdrawn. Another extreme case. Even now, after opening up to Bart somewhat, Sharon still

43

has a tendency to curl up into a tight ball on the seat of the bus, lowering her head between her legs and staring at the dark, dirty floor of the vehicle, her long, static-filled red hair concealing her freckled face. Though her movements are so few as to be almost nonexistent, she will furiously start punching anyone who tries to sit next to her. Most of the other kids don't try to anymore, but Bart will brave her clenched fists, giggling maniacally when Sharon lets loose on him, apparently feeling no pain as she strikes his shoulder again and again. One time he boldly ducked below her wild thrusts and tickled her in the ribs. This made her scream and cry, which so upset Bart that afterward he left her alone for a whole month.

Needless to say, after Bart dealt with Carl Spacklin, Sharon realized she had nothing to fear from her button-eating acquaintance, and she gladly surrendered half her seat to him. They've even begun talking.

Many of the kids on the bus for the emotionally disturbed are highly sensitive to an unusual variety of stimuli.

For instance, one morning Sharon cried all the way to the institute. This confused me, as nobody was bothering her. By the time we reached the institute, three other kids had decided to shed their tears along with her.

After I got all the other kids off the bus, I asked Ed to get off too. Cautiously I approached Sharon, who was rolled up like usual in her baggy green coat, her face buried, her back and shoulders heaving.

"What's wrong?" I asked her.

Some weeks earlier, she had started to converse with me when we were alone, but it was still an effort for her. Slowly she unfolded herself and pointed past her legs to the floor of the bus.

I looked and saw only caked dirt, and told her so.

She nodded in agreement. "But where's the Milky Way wrapper?" she said.

"It used to be there, but now it's gone!"

Someone at the maintenance garage had cleaned out the bus since yesterday afternoon's trip back to the school.

I was left wondering how one acclimatizes or helps make healthy children whose happiness depends on things like crumpled candy wrappers. It's a tough job, but I try to do my best.

My latest crop of emotionally disturbed students have gradually adjusted to one another, shaping for themselves a traveling microcosm — the bus — that operates, for the most part, on mutual respect. My kids aren't that different from those outside the bus; they laugh and cry and get angry, just like everybody else in this crazy world. The main difference is that my kids don't always emote at the proper times; they often chuckle at apparent tragedy or weep at what seems to be good fortune. Maybe that's why they're considered emotionally disturbed: their timing is off. And that's not such a big failing, really.

Our timing among ourselves has become pretty good. The kids know whom they can talk to and what their fellow students' interests and dislikes are. Some of them, like Sharon Fegley, are simply left alone. Nobody eats candy in front of Justin Mendoza. When Krystle Lambdin slides out of her seat, several kids dutifully rush to the front of the bus to help me put her back in it.

Wary of Bart and out of a sense of self-preservation, no one wears clothing with buttons — or if they do, the buttons are well concealed beneath zippered jackets or pullover sweaters.

Sometimes the kids exchange gifts. I join in on this ritual. In fact, on the day Button Eater became a hero, I brought him a present that thrilled him immensely: the latest issue of *Iron Man,* his favorite comic book. Tony Stark, the metal-suited crime fighter's alter ego, has a weak heart. I think that's why Button Eater admires him so much: he perceives that Iron Man is as flawed as he is. If famous defenders of justice can have coronary difficulties, then surely little boys can eat buttons.

"Oh, wow!" exclaimed Button Eater, snatching the comic book from my grasp the morning I brought it for him. "Thanks, Bernie!"

After making sure all the kids were in place and comfortable on the bus, I motioned for Ed to get going. I took my usual seat at the back of the bus, on the left side of the aisle.

Button Eater was already lost in the pages of *Iron Man,* totally oblivious to Sharon Fegley and everyone else. He was stretched out in his seat on the other side of the aisle, his back against the sloping window frame.

As we headed downtown, Krystle Lambdin unfastened the safety belt she so detested and slid right out onto the floor. It looked like this was not going to be one of her better days. Todd Hooley and Mindy O'Rourke hurried forward to return her to her custom-designed seat, and I made my way up to the front of the bus to assist.

Krystle's emotional problems had been accompanied by — or perhaps caused by — a congenital defect of her spine. In addition, her speaking ability was impaired; at age fourteen, she had only a three-year-old's mastery of verbal skills. When she was in one of her fouler moods, she would repeatedly unbuckle her safety belt, and her pudding-like spine could not prevent her from swirling to the floor of the bus like water down a drain. Her muscles and bones were soft and flexible enough that this habit caused her no pain or injury. Since she could barely talk or gesture at things, we had trouble understanding her when she tried to indicate why she was so upset. Unfortunately it was against state law to lock Krystle's buckle in such a way as to prevent her from opening it, and her specially designed seat took up so much room that nobody could sit directly beside her.

"Now Krystle," I said as Todd and Mindy buckled her in again, "you know it makes us very unhappy when you undo your safety belt while the bus is moving."

"Beat her fuckin' face in, coach!"

I spun around to face eleven-year-old Rodney Torgeson, wagging a finger at him. "We'll have no more talk like that, young man."

"Who's 'we,' coach? Only one I hear talking is <u>you.</u> And the only reason you don't cuss is 'cause you're a *pussy.*"

In Rodney's case, I had abandoned my dear Sigmund and subscribed to Adler's theory of aggression, which states that people behave violently in response to deeply rooted frustrations. I had not yet fully probed the source of Rodney's anxieties, but I knew he was my most difficult student as far as being willfully antisocial.

"Rodney," I said, remaining calm, "Krystle's got enough problems. Let's leave her face alone."

"Damn right she's got problems," he said. "Everybody on this bus has problems. Shit, I feel like killin' somebody."

"No you don't," I said. "What seems to be the matter today?"

"I'm having my period, coach."

"Don't get smart. And quit calling me 'coach.' I've told you time and time again not to call me that. I've never coached anything."

"I'll be smart if I want to," Rodney declared. "Isn't that why we go to this God-damned nuthouse school? To get smart?"

"Rodney!" snapped Button Eater, lowering his comic book. "Just shut up!"

Rodney stared at Button Eater in disbelief, shocked that one of his peers was courageous enough to challenge him. After a long pause, Rodney pretended to be chewing something as he said, "Haven't you got some buttons to eat?"

47

I returned to my seat at the back of the bus, having decided to wait and deal with Rodney once we arrived at the institute.

A few moments later, Carl Spacklin forced himself onto the bus.

Ed had stopped at a red light, and I could see him looking to his right, out the front door of the bus. Clearly someone or something had captured his attention. Ed opened the door partway, maintaining his hold on the metal handle. The man who turned out to be Spacklin kicked the door all the way in, fracturing Ed's wrist in the process, and stomped on board, pulling a revolver from his jacket pocket as he yelled, "I'm hijacking this bus!"

"This is a bus for emotionally disturbed children," replied Ed, as if being in such a category made our vehicle impervious to hostile takeover. Ed cradled his injured right hand like a newborn baby, wincing every so often.

"Doesn't matter," said Spacklin, "as long as we get there."

"Get where?" asked Ed.

"The Middle East." Spacklin pointed the gun at Ed's temple as if daring him to argue. Ed chose not to inform Spacklin that the aging bus would be performing a miracle merely to last as far as the state line, let alone cross the Atlantic Ocean.

Spacklin's intense, fixation-pause gaze betrayed the sordid inner turmoil of the hopelessly psychotic. He was not paranoid, as best I could determine this early on. He had simply lost touch with reality and was unable to discern even the most fundamental meanings of what occurred around him.

"What country?" inquired Ed.

"Doesn't matter," Spacklin said. "Just drive. I'll take care of business when I get there."

"'Business'?"

"Well, you know," he said, sounding almost grateful to be able to outline his plans, "those damned camel jockeys are always causing trouble, always wanting

48

to *kill.* We, the Haganah, will take care of things."

The Haganah, I later found out, was a terrorist group in the Middle East. I'm sure Spacklin never belonged to that organization.

"Are you going to shoot anybody?" asked Ed.

"Here or over there?" As Ed appeared to struggle with an appropriate response to Spacklin's query, the latter man continued: "You know, you ask a lot of questions for a guy who could get killed real easy."

"Now hold on," I said, rising to my feet. "There's no need to harm anybody on this bus."

Spacklin's dark eyes swung in my direction. "Who are you? Are you in charge here?"

"Well, yes," I said, figuring somebody had to be, so it might as well be me.

"Tell your driver to put this junk heap in gear," said Spacklin.

I didn't want Spacklin killing anybody, especially one of my kids, most of whom were cringing in terror. (Their timing was improving!) So I decided playing along with Spacklin was, at this point, the safest course of action.

Ed was waiting for my instructions.

"Head east," I told him.

"Bernie, I'm running low on gas," Ed informed me.

"That's okay, Ed. We'll fill up before we get to Georgia."

Spacklin moved threateningly toward me. "Was that some kind of a joke or what?"

"No!" I said, taking a step back and reminding myself to keep my sarcasm in check. Maybe Spacklin was more paranoid than I thought.

The armed psycho grabbed the collar of Sharon Fegley's ugly coat and pulled her toward him. She squealed briefly but kept her face hidden in the crook of her arm. He pressed his gun against the back of her skull.

"I'll decorate this bus with her brains if I have to," he said, glaring at me.

"Yeah!" cheered Rodney Torgeson. "My kind of guy!"

Spacklin looked at Rodney. "What the fuck's the matter with you, kid?"

"Please!" I exclaimed. "Sharon is harmless. Don't shoot her. We don't mean to cause you any trouble."

Spacklin took another step in my direction.

That final step was his undoing.

Correction: wearing a jacket with buttons was his undoing.

Southpaw Spacklin halted next to the seat occupied by Button Eater. The hand that grasped his gun extended out of a sleeve adorned with two buttons.

It had been weeks since Bart had seen a button. This unexpected feast was even more exciting than the new *Iron Man*.

Before Spacklin knew what was happening, Button Eater lunged at him, teeth bared. As he gnawed on Spacklin's jacket sleeve, the gunman lost his grip on Sharon Fegley, dropping her to the aisle of the bus. She rolled up into her customary spherical self. Spacklin tried to switch the gun to his other hand, but in doing so, the weapon fired and flew out of his reach. I heard Button Eater's cry of anguish, then felt a sharp pain in my right foot. I managed to fall on top of the gun as four of the boys helped Button Eater tackle Spacklin.

The bullet had ricocheted off Button Eater's ear and lodged in my foot, but at least nobody had been killed.

Rodney Torgeson looked down at Spacklin, shaking his head. "Nice going, you asshole," he said, sounding almost disappointed that Spacklin's criminal agenda had been foiled.

I observed an interaction I would never have thought possible: Sharon Fegley unrolled herself, pulled the bleeding Button Eater to her, and kissed him delicately on the cheek.

Successes like that one go a long way toward explaining why riding the bus for the emotionally disturbed isn't always as bad as it might seem to outsiders.

Kent Robinson

Our justice system requires jurors to follow the law and the dictates of the court as established by the judge in each case. In addition, I believe jurors need to follow their hearts and their common-sense understanding of what is right when the law and the judge's instructions still leave a gray area as to how to ultimately decide a case.

Bledsoe, the main character in this story, certainly does not perform his duty as a juror in the way he knows he should.

I once served on a jury on which a fellow juror was asleep most of the time. The judge periodically hollered at him to wake him up. It was hard for me to see how the guy could make a good decision as to the guilt or innocence of the defendant.

One final note: you'll discover that the lady lawyer in this story does the right thing. Who says all lawyers are cretins?

JUSTICE IS BLEDSOE'S

The court clerk — an innocent-eyed Hispanic woman with a tomboy haircut and an endlessly smiling mouth too large for her face — waves the thirty potential jurors into the courtroom, where they are instructed to sit in the audience section. This remark is offered without explanation, and Bledsoe isn't sure which section she means. Nevertheless, he copes without any observable panic; he makes his way by following the potential jurors ahead of him, filing into a row of brown seats directly behind a fat woman with oily red hair who insists on offering her opinions of everything, no matter how insignificant or personal the topic. Whereas the rest of the potential jurors seem to have learned to block out the woman's remarks, Bledsoe finds himself unable to stop listening to her, and that, in and of itself, annoys him, not to mention the agitation he experiences over the nature of her blathering.

"These seats sure aren't made for comfort's sake," she complains the moment Bledsoe sits down next to her.

Bledsoe hears her, understands her words, does not entirely disagree with her assessment of the furniture, but declines to respond. It would only encourage her to say something else. Instead he leans forward and scans the front of the room, noting plaintiff's and defendant's tables. A bearded court recorder sits behind his cluttered desk along the far right wall of the room, manipulating writing instruments and other office supplies. The whole room — furnishings and floor and ceiling and paneling — exudes brown tones.

The clerk calls the court to order and makes everyone rise. Judge Cromwell, a huge, lumbering man who easily weighs 250 pounds, enters the courtroom, takes his seat at the bench, and appears to sort confusedly through a stack of papers, blocking out all else as if he is the only person present in the room. He looks to be about sixty years old and wears a hairpiece and glasses that do not become him. However, he seems unconcerned about his appearance, and Bledsoe is impressed by this. Score one for the judge, he thinks. Generally Bledsoe tends to admire a lack of self-consciousness in authority figures.

The clerk finishes her anthem about the seriousness of the proceedings soon to be undertaken, and then everybody sits back down.

"This is the case," reads Cromwell in a gravelly voice, "of Bess Sanasarian vs. Wilhelm Medical Enterprises, Wilhelm General Hospital Inc., and the Amalgamated Group of Wilhelm Medical." He looks from paper to counsels. "Is that right?"

Already, Bledsoe thinks idly, poor Bess Sanasarian has lost the case. How can one person hope to stand up against a bunch of enterprises, a corporation, and an amalgamation? Or are the odds not really so stacked against her? When you get right down to it, he knows, each case is ultimately person against person, right against wrong, deception against clarity. Though he has never served on a jury, he imagines the odds are always more even than one might at first believe. The twenty-nine other potential jurors might disagree with him, but he doesn't care. He'll bring objectivity and intelligence to these proceedings, while they, on the other hand, will more than likely be helpless in their efforts to employ either. If you could peel away their layers of ignorance, you would no doubt find that *objectivity,* like *individuality* or *responsibility,* strikes them as some sort of foreign or theoretical concept, a word they claim to *know the meaning of* and are *in favor of* but at the same time are powerless to plug in to the sockets of their daily lives in any workable fashion.

Bledsoe scans the other potential jurors, a process he began while standing in the hallway among them. He derives much more pleasure from looking at them than he ever could from talking to them. He is searching, in particular, for good-looking women. To his surprise, he discovers three of them in the group, two blondes and a brunette. Each is at least five feet eight inches tall — *tall,* the way he usually likes his women, being the operative word — and two of the three have marvelously thin, well-sculpted faces. The third woman's face is distractingly round, but her smile is nicer, and she most likely has the finest legs of the trio, judging by what Bledsoe has been able to see of their lower appendages from their ankles to the glorious region several inches above their knees.

The rest of the women obviously have severe problems with diet or disproportion or attitude, and Bledsoe ignores them. He glances at the faces of the men and sees no one as handsome as himself or even as interesting looking as the ugliest woman. This surprises him, since he doesn't regard himself as handsome. Nonetheless, the other men appear used up or somehow stupid or gawky (that last, as with some of the women, being a proportional quandary), and, as a result, he feels himself shining through, taking the prize, looking impressive. Surely, he thinks, if anyone in this courtroom is going to get laid as this trial plods along, it's going to be me.

One by one the judge calls the potential jurors up into the box, where the lawyers question them. Each lawyer has the right to dismiss ten potential jurors without having to give the judge a reason, and the defendant's counsel, specifically, seems eager to exercise this right. Plaintiff's attorney, though, is more accepting of the jurors who are called, and she is forced to question lots of people only because the other side repeatedly says, "Your honor, I would thank the juror and ask that [s]he be dismissed."

Bledsoe does not pay close attention to the plaintiff's attorney until he is called into the box. For one thing, up until then he has been able to observe her only from behind. Once in the box, however, he notices that Margaret Dixon is not entirely unattractive. The more he stares at her, the more convinced he is that here is a sexual volcano waiting to erupt, who longs to spread herself to the blissful fulfillment of surrender and penetration.

No one is more amazed than Bledsoe himself when he is approved as a member of the jury in the case of Sanasarian vs. Wilhelm Medical Enterprises, Wilhelm General Hospital Services Inc., and the Amalgamated Group of Wilhelm Medical. After all, he has been rejected in five other cases and had virtually abandoned the idea of ever actually getting the opportunity to serve.

To his dismay, one of the blondes has been questioned and dismissed. The other two women whom Bledsoe finds attractive do not even get a chance to be questioned, as a full jury is formed before their names are called. Bledsoe grimly notes that three of the seven women on the jury are grossly overweight and include the generously opinionated redhead. Two others are unsightly Asians, and the remaining pair — one African American, one Caucasian — seem perpetually glum, appearing exhausted by lives that are probably uninspired and directionless. The black woman's mini-skirt reveals that she does have something going for her in the legs department, but her face is permanently contorted into some exaggerated expression of inner agony that prohibits Bledsoe from generating any lust.

This is just great, thinks Bledsoe as he sits among his fellow jurors. What did I do to deserve this? Just my luck to get selected with a bunch of singularly unapproachable genetic defects. Bledsoe gnaws his lip and adjusts a leg of his pants. He could have gotten out of serving, he knows. All he would have had to do is state some incredible bias against anything, and he would have been on his way back to the assembly room with the three gorgeous women. Right now he could have been arranging some sort of game plan, with one or more of the three women, for the weekend.

He focuses again on Margaret Dixon. Here is possibility. She wears a wedding ring, but these days that means almost nothing. When she questioned him minutes ago, that look in her eyes told him — or at the very least he told himself — that she is at a crossroads in her life where she is destined to take the route of infidelity. Her husband isn't working out; perhaps he's incompetent in the sack or is fooling around himself or is, to an increasingly disappointing degree, not the man she thought she was marrying when that event took place. Bledsoe doesn't know and doesn't care. But by God if he's forced to sit here in this courtroom for the next ten days, he's going to make it worth his while, he's going to accomplish something, going to move in on this lady lawyer. He is just the man she's been waiting for. Now that she's seen and talked to him, the lawyer's concern for the fate of her client or for the achievement of justice in any kind of larger sense is at this point only remotely operative. The case will start soon, the facts or warped interpretations thereof will be presented, and a ruling will be handed down, but either way, defendant's and plaintiff's legal representatives will receive their inflated fees, so what do they care? Decision is almost beside the point.

Then again, thinks Bledsoe, it's always easier to get your next client and demand even higher amounts of money when you can boast a winning record, so in the long-term sense of her microcosmic career, winning is crucial.

Judge Cromwell is speaking. In the case of Bess Sanasarian vs. Wilhelm Medical Enterprises, Wilhelm General Hospital Services Inc., and the Amalgamated Group of Wilhelm Medical, it would appear that a Wilhelm employee under Sanasarian's direct supervision got her car scratched while it was unattended in the Wilhelm parking structure on Santa Monica Boulevard. An eyewitness claims to have seen a woman fitting Sanasarian's description commit the vandalism. In addition, a security guard says he saw Sanasarian exit the parking structure at about the time of the incident. Sanasarian seems to have possessed motive, as she had for months been complaining to her boss that she was having trouble supervising the nurse with the scratched car and suspected the woman was out to get her job. Sanasarian was eventually terminated from her $50,000-a-year position as Wilhelm's emergency nursing supervisor. Plaintiff is challenging the firing and, due to difficulties she's had finding employment since then, is seeking $225,000 in damages.

The next day plaintiff's and defendant's counsels offer their opening statements. They speak of the former nursing supervisor, Sanasarian, in the past tense, as if she is dead. Sanasarian was a model employee, a hard worker, well educated, a loving mother, a loyal wife, falsely accused. Sanasarian was impatient, inefficient under stress, vengeful, constantly whining to her superiors about the most insignificant of problems, divorced once before her current marriage, unmistakably the person who had taken out her frustrations with her least favorite nurse by using a key to scratch that nurse's car.

Eye contact.

Bledsoe knows eye contact with a woman is meaningful. He is pleased to have established, at least intermittently, such contact with Margaret Dixon. She glances at him from time to time. He's sure that she knows what he is thinking, what he wants, and he feels certain it's exactly what she wants too.

Dixon is a few inches shorter than the model types who'd been among the pool of potential jurors, but Bledsoe is willing to accept that. He's never made love to an attorney, and his fantasies involving Dixon have caused her to blossom, in his mind, into a goddess to be seduced. Normally he likes women with long, wavy hair, but Dixon's short, curly locks are perfect for her face. Her eyes are active and aware, her nose thin and well defined. Bledsoe is certain, in analyzing Dixon's calves and making projections on the basis of their length and shape, that her thighs are every bit as luscious as the brunette's of a few days ago, if slightly shorter. Dixon wears glasses, which accentuate her intelligent look. Her lips are thin but not hard. Bledsoe imagines his own mouth pressing against those lips, tasting her breath, his hands sliding from her waist up to the outer regions of her breasts as her fingers dance nervously upon his biceps. He gently places her on her back atop the short wall that separates the jurors from the main floor of the court-room. her limbs fall to either side of the wall as Bledsoe pushes her skirt up, up, steadily, confidently, his palms kneading the malleable flesh of her inner legs, her eyes dreamy and only half open, her thoughts already wafting onto a distant plain of ecstasy, her head rolling slowly left and right as low groans begin to escape her throat from the deep interior —

Defendant's counsel slaps the podium, snapping Bledsoe out of his reverie. This lawyer, a beady-eyed, oily-skinned man named Gilford, is questioning a witness originally called to the stand by Dixon. Gilford is doing his best to emasculate the man with dignity and charm.

The witness, a baby-faced fellow named Bellinger, is a private investigator from Sacramento. Dixon has used Bellinger to pick apart the shoddy and hasty investigation of Sanasarian implemented by Wilhelm administrators immediately prior to the nursing supervisor's dismissal. Now Gilford is attacking Bellinger — his credentials, his work history, his personal quirks — in an attempt to nullify the investigator's previous testimony by hurling calumniations.

Again Gilford strikes the side of the podium. *"So!"* he yells. "Before this court you go so far as to render an opinion of Wilhelm's investigation *without ever having read the full deposition of the Wilhelm security chief!"*

It's noisy, but even so, Bledsoe, who regards Gilford as the sort of lawyer who gives the legal profession a bad name, is unable to keep his mind on the legal proceedings at the moment. The insinuative pitch of Gilford's voice is irritating, but Bledsoe concentrates on Dixon, imagining the precise curves of her body's clothed areas as she sits next to her assistants and her client and feverishly takes notes. Bledsoe wishes she would glance over at him, flash him one of her smiles, but he understands that this trial does represent the essence of her livelihood, and concerns unrelated to him are temporarily in control of her attention.

The court clerk with the expansive mouth has provided each juror with a notepad and a pencil. Bledsoe flips open his pad and scans the twenty pages of so-called notes. After six days of trial, not counting today, he finds that his scribblings pertaining to this civil case consist of more than fifty crude renderings of the Hanna-Barbera creation Fred Flintstone, the beginning of what reads like a superficial diary entry, various geometric designs (predominantly cubes), and naked tits, which suddenly strike Bledsoe as being wonderfully geometric in their own way, and certainly more exciting than cubes.

Turning to a clean page, he neatly prints the following: LET'S DO LUNCH. CALL ME. He includes his phone number and signs his name. Carefully and quietly he tears the page out of the pad.

It's about time we get this show on the road, he thinks. At the upcoming break, he will slip her the note as he glides past her on his way out of the courtroom.

The following morning Bledsoe enters the courtroom in a bad mood. Margaret Dixon hasn't called, and he is upset. As he ascends a flight of stairs leading up to the fifth floor, he finds himself, quite by accident, alongside the obese redhead who is serving on the jury with him.

Christ, he thinks, the last thing I need today is to hear a bunch of crap from her. She is barely tolerable even under the best of circumstances, and given his current emotional state, he doesn't know if he can survive her neurotic, unstructured ramblings.

Immediately she starts in.

"Why couldn't they have this stupid trial on the first floor, God, I hate walking up these steps each morning, I think they do it on purpose just because they like to make things difficult for people, how long is the elevator going to be out of order, that's the government for you, you'd think they could plan things a little bit better, and these lousy steps couldn't be any steeper — "

"Shut up," mutters Bledsoe, waving his hands in exasperation at the sides of his head, "just keep your mouth shut for a change. Can you manage that? You're constantly fucking talking. I don't want to listen to you babble on endlessly."

The redhead is shocked at his reaction, but Bledsoe is unremorseful. He is sick and tired of her. She is so pitifully common in perceiving herself as the important, abused center of some kind of harsh universe, where "they" are inferior, bumbling, "stupid," but apparently, through sheer willpower, repeatedly succeed in "making things difficult" for her. However, "they" never seem to be actually, physically present; if indeed "they" are, she obviously doesn't care whether "they" overhear her, since she speaks indiscriminately to anybody or any object in her vicinity. "They" are at once everyone and no one, everything and nothing. People like her, Bledsoe has noticed over the years, invariably have no inkling as to how hopelessly stupid and contradictory *they* themselves are.

He quickly puts some distance between himself and the redhead as he makes his way to the fifth floor, where he passes through the empty courtroom and takes a seat in the adjoining waiting room. The rest of the jurors, alternate included, have already arrived. Minutes later the redhead heaves herself into the room, struggling for breath as she glares at Bledsoe.

Before she has a chance to sit down, the court clerk pokes her head inside the room to tell them the judge is ready to begin. Solemnly they go into the courtroom, where, almost as if by magic, everyone save for the judge has appeared. Once the jurors have taken their seats, the black-robed Cromwell strides in as the clerk calls the court to order. The judge says good morning and adjusts himself behind the bench. He notices one of the jurors has a thick paperback resting on the railing in front of her, and he asks her about it; they discuss the book, and literature in general, for several minutes, oblivious to their surroundings. Throughout the trial Cromwell has seemed far more interested in exchanging small talk with the jurors and telling quaint jokes prior to the breaks than absorbing the details of Bess Sanasarian's plight. Bledsoe is amused by this and increasingly feels that the judge is the only person in the entire room whom he truly likes.

Only after Cromwell and the juror are done talking does Bledsoe bother to glance at Margaret Dixon. As well as being angry, he is embarrassed by the fact that she did not call. She is busy going over some document with one of her assistants. As a whole, the trial has been comically marred by improperly processed papers, nonfunctioning videotape machines, and lights and an air-conditioning unit that seem to operate with technological free will, giving the judge plenty of inspiration for sarcastic asides about the mechanical trappings of modern-day justice.

Bledsoe stares at Dixon for several minutes, but she refuses to look his way. I've alienated her, he thinks. I should have waited until after the trial to move in on her. She wants me as badly as I want her, I'm positive of it, but she also wants to win the case. She doesn't want to jeopardize the case by having someone spot us together. Well, fuck the case. Some things just cannot wait. I won't be ignored. Maybe I rushed this thing some, okay, pardon me, but it's too late to turn back now. Remember your useless husband, Ms. Dixon. You, like I, have no choice but to move ahead and satisfy your carnal appetite.

Poor little Bess Sanasarian. In her case against Wilhelm Medical Enterprises, Wilhelm General Hospital Services Inc., and the Amalgamated Group of Wilhelm Medical, all the evidence seems to indicate that her rights as nursing supervisor were utterly and appallingly violated. She was fired within twenty-four hours of the report of the car scratching, and that report came from a single eyewitness, an eyewitness who, according to the Wilhelm attorney, did not know Sanasarian at the time of the incident and thus had nothing to gain by blowing the whistle on her. But most probably, thinks Bledsoe, the eyewitness has known and disliked Sanasarian and is now lying, oath be damned, while the weaselly Gilford, a stranger to ethic, will say anything, support any veracity, on behalf of his monolithic client, Wilhelm.

Bledsoe knows that Sanasarian is innocent. he feels it in his gut. While her behavior on the stand did reveal a palpable impatience when her response to complex questions failed to meet with easy understanding — not the most terrific characteristic in a supervisor — she never gave any impression of being vindictive

63

enough to damage a co-worker's vehicle. Some well-insulated, upper-level Wilhelm bureaucrat no doubt had it in for the nursing supervisor and was determined to ruin her career upon being informed of the crime.

Bledsoe scans the other jurors, one by one, as they gaze with moronic paralysis at whoever happens to be speaking. He wonders how clear the truth is to them. They are, after all, dimwitted to a severe degree, very likely not comprehending most of what is happening. Perhaps they view it as appropriate that Sanasarian was charged with the crime. They consider her evil. Bledsoe is aware that evil, the concept of evil, plays a big role in the psychological makeup of a number of the jurors; having noted the reading material and overheard wisps of conversations, he knows that three of the jurors, possibly four, are born-again Christians. (With a grim chuckle Bledsoe wonders if these individuals *aborted* their previous selves to become born again.) Intellectually crippled by phantoms of their past, they are quick to paint reality in the starkly contrasting colors of sinful or saintly. For instance, Bledsoe knows they consider him someone to stay away from, someone evil maybe, at the very least someone too argumentative and sarcastic. And this holy trio does not even include the unstable redhead, who despises him after his remarks to her on the stairs a few days ago.

He dismisses the jurors, as it were, from his mind and opens his notepad. On a clean page he again puts down his phone number and name. We'll try again, he thinks. She simply needs an additional nudge.

While he goes through his mail that evening at the office, the phone rings. Eagerly he picks up the receiver and says hello.

"Mr. Bledsoe, you know who this is," Margaret Dixon says tersely. "I thought I had better call you. While I am flattered at your interest in me, I think you should know that I am happily married and don't want to get involved with you. Let's just get through this trial, do what we're supposed to do in the courtroom, and then go our separate ways." She falls silent, and Bledsoe remains that way. He doesn't know what to say.

She hangs up.

By late the next morning, plaintiff's and defendant's counsels complete their closing statements. Margaret Dixon does her best to portray Bess Sanasarian as an innocent victim, a capable employee whose professional career has been scarred, if not obliterated, by the insensitive giant that is Wilhelm. Gilford asserts that Wilhelm's investigation was thorough, that Sanasarian was becoming increasingly unmanageable as a worker, and that she exhibited her final act of recalcitrance, as far as Wilhelm is concerned, on the day she damaged another employee's property.

Bledsoe rises and files with the rest of the jurors into the waiting room, where they will deliberate. Before today this would have been the most painful part of his jury service as he's imagined it, descending to the level of these fools in an attempt to render a verdict. But now he is looking forward to it, he finds himself motivated by purpose. Bess Sanasarian, if she is a vengeful person, isn't the only one, he thinks.

The trial has lasted twelve days, not ten, as originally estimated, but only a few minutes after taking their seats in the waiting room, the eleven other jurors emphatically state their decisions in the case. No, each of them seems to be indicating, if Bledsoe gauges their moods correctly, I don't want to debate it, I've made up my mind, let's not spend the rest of our lives quibbling in this courtroom, I've got a job and a family and Dodgers tickets and various duties, and that's final. Typical of the insufferably close-minded, thinks Bledsoe. Oddly the redhead appears least anxious to voice her opinion, which makes Bledsoe want to both laugh at her and smack her.

Three of the jurors conclude that Wilhelm is guilty as charged in the suit filed by Sanasarian. Eight of them believe that Sanasarian is lying, that she lacks numerous essential qualities of the truly skilled supervisor, and that events relating to her job eventually overwhelmed her, permeating her professional façade and causing her to damage the car. The born-again Christians are the ones who find enough mercy within themselves to side with Sanasarian. That figures, thinks Bledsoe. Even if the nursing supervisor deserved to be fired, the Bible wavers are exactly the type to find forgiveness in their hearts, to indulge in a sort of spiritual ejaculation as they replace their god with themselves for the purpose of doling out a department store version of almighty acquittal.

Well, not me, he thinks, pounding the table. The other jurors turn toward him, many of them reluctantly, a few others perhaps wondering if he's suffering a spasm as a result of some obscure medical problem. Sanasarian may not have scratched the car, but then again, then again, maybe she did. Bledsoe knows she didn't, his gut holds true on the matter. But so what? She is represented by a lawyer who thinks she can lead me on, can toy with me. Margaret Dixon regards me as putty in her hands, as a dolt to be teased and swayed for her own purposes.

"She's lying," says Bledsoe, "Sanasarian is lying through her teeth," and he doesn't wish to argue about his decision either. His hopes of getting it on with Margaret Dixon have long since faded away, like echoes down a canyon pass. He realizes Dixon needs him to decide in Sanasarian's favor in order to win the case. "Bess Sanasarian is lying, she scratched the car, you can be sure of it."

The editor of the magazine that originally published this story rejected an earlier submission of mine, saying he was looking for "party" stories for the upcoming issue. In other words, the issue was going to be what is referred to in publishing as a theme *issue, with the theme being parties. My favorite pro football team, the Green Bay Packers, had just won the Super Bowl, so I wrote and sent him "Bears in the Punch Bowl," which he accepted.*

If you follow football, you may already suspect that the "Bears" part of this story's title may not necessarily refer to the furry, lumbering beasts that walk around on all fours. (Then again, maybe it does!)

The magazine this story appeared in was Words of Wisdom. *As far as I can tell, there's no wisdom in the story, but what do I know? Story does have a cool title, however, playful and bouncy, which is why I made it the name of this book.*

Incidentally, my favorite college football team, in case you were wondering, is the University of Southern California (USC) Trojans.

BEARS IN THE PUNCH BOWL

January 26 — Super Bowl Sunday — had finally arrived. Even with temperatures well below the freezing mark, our hearts were warmed by the knowledge that the Chicago Bears had failed miserably in their efforts to secure an NFL playoff berth, let alone make it to today's big dance. Duh Bears! The only team we came close to hating as much as the Bears was the Dallas Cowboys. *America's* team. Cue laughter.

The holidays were behind us. Visions of dancing sugarplums — a peculiar concept if ever there was one — had been replaced by far more sublime images, like a determined Desmond Howard returning kickoffs for TDs or a sideswiping Reggie White knocking offensive linemen on their surprised butts as he slavered in pursuit of a scrambling Drew Bledsoe.

The Pack was back. The Green Bay Packers, that is. This hadn't been just another year in which diehard cheeseheads had made that statement until December, only to have the bitter chill of its untruthfulness seep into their frigid, frustrated bones. No, this time the Pack's backness was definitely a reality. They were in the Super Bowl!

Joe and Suzanne Mackey's house, in the hushed, frozen countryside surrounding Elkhart, Indiana, was in noticeable disarray, not only because of strewn winter coats, empty beer bottles, and widely scattered munchies of the forty or so partygoers in attendance but also due to extensive remodeling. The scuffed linoleum and tattered carpeting were history, but new hadn't yet replaced the old. Wood destined to be turned into cabinets was stacked haphazardly in a corner of the dining room, next to where the microwave was located. Cups and plates and mugs not in use — many with big Packer Gs emblazoned proudly upon them — were stored in odd nooks and crannies, wherever there was room. The dog biscuits were placed on high so Luther and Sadie wouldn't tear into them when nobody was looking. Buster could still reach the canine treats and might very well do so before the evening ended, but he was one of the adult humans, so he could do what he wanted.

Pre-game bullshit blared from strategically placed televisions in the bedrooms, kitchen, dining room, and living room, where the big-screen Zenith, glowing formidably in a corner, held the attention of zealous football fans like a kind of holy altar upon which a virgin sacrifice was about to be performed, a description not altogether erroneous, though the New England Patriots weren't exactly virgins, having played in — and lost — Super Bowl XX.

"Where's Gordon?" asked Pam, a bug-eyed blonde with frenziedly moving elbows that always seemed to be lashing out at anyone near her. The motion of bringing a beer can or potato chip to her lips was a warning to those close by that they were in danger. She wore a gray sweatshirt decorated with a green, oval-shaped G bordered by yellow trim.

"He's not here yet," responded a woman I couldn't see on the other side of the dining room from Pam. I was in the living room, drinking my fifth or sixth brewskie and munching pretzels as I got comfy in the antique rocker located close to the big screen. Terry and Howie were clowning around in the studio while, in the background, a camera panned across the parking lot outside the Louisiana Superdome, where numerous tailgate parties were in full swing. Luther and Sadie were patrolling everywhere with single-minded purpose, seeking edible handouts, their claws clicking against naked flooring. Luther was a black and white Boston terrier, and wire-haired Sadie was a temperamental, street-smart mutt.

Even though it was Joe and Suzanne's house and Luther and Sadie were their dogs, Gordon and Julie Stinson's pets were destined to become our unofficial Packers mascots: two handsome, densely muscled male Rottweilers, barely beyond the puppy stage, named Lambeau and Lombardi. Contrary to the breed's popular image, Lambeau and Lombardi were friendly, as long as they knew the person and didn't get teased or laughed at too much. They were, however, somewhat reckless in their movements, frequently running into cupboards or hitting their heads on furniture without seeming to notice and apparently without suffering any ill effects. The temperature outside was a mere five degrees above zero, so the Stinsons would undoubtedly arrive with the canines clad in their custom-made Packers dog coats, which made them look both charming and silly.

None of us was overly superstitious, but I'm almost sure that on a level not too far below the verbal, more than a few in attendance — including me — fretted over the irrational idea that it would be bad luck for anybody to show up after the opening kickoff, now less than half an hour away. Especially Gordon, who, during the regular season, had occasionally arrived at Joe and Suzanne's with something less than punctuality. We'd reached the beer-blurred, stubbornly sloppy conclu-sion (not necessarily supported by the facts) that those games were, more often than not, losses for the Pack or, at best, frighteningly close games or costly ones in terms of injuries. The contest that sidelined Brooks for the season? Gordon's pickup truck had run out of gas, and he'd arrived fifteen minutes late.

"Hopefully there'll be some good commercials," said Jeff from one end of a couch as he grabbed the brim of his Packers cap and rubbed the inner lining back and forth over his broad, likely itchy forehead.

"Probably lots of beer ads," predicted his pretty sister, Tawny, from the couch's other end.

"There'd better be a new Cindy Crawford commercial," blurted Ed, "or I'll be pissed!"

"Oh, brother," said Tawny, rolling her dark, shiny eyes.

Blond, four-year-old Devon relinquished his grip on his mother's leg and strolled into the living room from the dining room. He was dressed in a Packers cap, a Favre jersey, and Packers sweats: a young cheesehead in the making, being molded with loving care greater than that applied to the most scrumptious block of Swiss. Sporting a happy smile, Devon wandered over to me, extended a tiny hand that held a Yak Bak, and pushed the PLAY button. "Go, Packers!" issued his voice from the plastic toy, and everyone laughed. For as long as he held the button down, the cheer kept repeating.

"Save my seat," I told Devon, getting up and lifting the boy onto the padded leather cushion. "Be right back. I'll bring you a cookie."

"Go, Packers!" blustered the Yak Bak. "Go, Packers!"

I waded through the crowd in the dining room and kitchen, greeting new arriv-als and high-fiving the raised palms of familiar people. I asked Steve how his '77 T-bird was running, then exchanged some sick humor with P. J.

"If two lesbians and two queers traveled from point A to point B," asked P. J., inhaling a Coors, "who would arrive first?"

"Beats me."

"The lesbians, 'cause the queers would have to pack their shit."

"Okay, I got one." Then I paused awkwardly for a few seconds, staring off into space as if I were only now hearing the joke when in fact I was simply trying to remember it accurately. "Um, okay, here it is. A guy walks into a tavern and sees another guy sitting at the bar with a fairly large box in front of him. Music is coming from the box. 'What's in there?' asks the guy who's just entered. 'Check it out,' says the other fellow. So the curious guy lifts the lid off the box and looks inside, where he sees a small man playing a piano. 'Wow, that's interesting,' he says. 'Where'd you get that?' The seated guy points to the other end of the bar and says, 'See that magic lamp down there? If you rub it, a genie will pop out and grant you one wish. He gave me this man in the box.' 'Really?' says the other guy, and without further ado he walks to the other end of the bar and rubs the lamp. Out pops the genie, who says, 'Your wish is my command. What would you like?' 'A million bucks!' says the guy. But instead of a million dollars appearing, the tavern suddenly fills with a million <u>ducks,</u> quacking like mad and fluttering all over the place. Immediately the genie disappears, so the guy goes back to the seated man and says, "That's a fine how-do-you-do. I wished for a million bucks, but that stupid genie gave me a million ducks instead.' 'Well,' says the other guy, 'you don't think I wished for a twelve-inch pianist, do you?'"

Eventually I made it to the other side of the house. A doorway led out to a small stoop, down which you cautiously made your way over slippery patches of snow and ice en route to the little entrance to the garage, ten feet away, where all the alcohol was stored. Needless to say, on game days this short route was heavily trafficked. Years ago Joe and Suzanne had acquired an old Coca-Cola

71

machine, dilapidated but functional. In it they stored long-necked bottles of Miller Lite. Scattered throughout the garage were guests' Styrofoam coolers, crammed with countless brands of beer; bottles of golden champagne sitting on the flat, hard surface of an electric table saw and waiting to be uncorked in a raucous victory celebration; and, rented from a local catering service especially for today, a hundred-gallon crystal punch bowl filled to the brim with spiked red drink. The temperature in the garage was low enough that the Coke cooler and polystyrene containers weren't necessary for keeping beverages chilled — witness the bottles of champagne, which you had only to touch to determine that their contents were lip-numbingly frigid, or the punch, where jagged ice slivers formed on the scarlet surface during rare stretches when ladle plunges were few and far between — but most of the booze had been brought here in handy carrying containers, and in those containers it would remain until it was drank.

Angela and Lisa were giggling on the far side of the punch bowl, balancing themselves by gripping the rim with one gloved hand each while hoisting drinks to mouths with their free hands. Their white breath blossomed into the shadowy air above them. Angela was wearing a Packers winter coat that must have cost at least a hundred dollars, and Lisa had on a Packers scarf and Packers stocking cap. Behind the two women, set into the west wall of the garage, was a window frame with no glass in it. Gazing through the empty square, I could see a row of a dozen or so vehicles parked roughly parallel to the garage, filling a large section of the yard.

"Randy!" Angela called, releasing the punch bowl to wave at me. She staggered backward, the inadvertent motion causing her to erupt with laughter.

Lisa, laughing also, raised her drink and yelled, "How randy are you?" This remark generated still more, and louder, laughter.

Dennis, Stan, and a redheaded woman in Packers earmuffs whose name I didn't know entered the garage in search of beer.

"You ladies gonna need a designated driver?" Stan asked Angela and Lisa, and we all busted a gut over that one. Everybody of legal age would be drunk as hell by the end of the night, and nobody would give a shit. You'd find no preaching, no political correctness, no unwanted busybodies here.

The men and Red Hot — as I'd begun to think of the beautiful, unidentified redhead — retrieved a Budweiser, a Coors, and a Honey Brown from their respective containers. I pulled a Miller Lite from the rusty Coke cooler.

I followed Dennis, Stan, and Red Hot back inside the house, immersing myself once more in a sea of green-, yellow-, and gray-clad bodies. Red Hot had a wonderfully shapely ass inside her tight jeans and a nice set of long legs accentuated to the point of distraction by a pair of fur-topped, shiny red boots that came up to just below her knees. I wondered who she was, but I'd already stumbled too far down the path leading to the blissful Kingdom of Inebriation to work up much sexual excitement about anyone or anything. Maybe I'd meet Red Hot later, maybe not. There were a dozen or so other people at the party whose names I didn't know and whose faces I didn't recognize. Friends brought friends, who sometimes brought friends who brought friends.... It was hard to keep track.

I paused at one of the numerous snack tables and grabbed a Chips Ahoy! for Devon, as promised. What the heck, he was a swell kid, so I got him two. He popped out of my chair and reached toward me for his treat as I reentered the living room. "Randy likes the Packers!" squawked the freshly made recording on his Yak Bak. "Randy likes the Packers!"

"Yes, I do," I said, delivering my best imitation of the smarmy guy on a beer commercial we all liked as I sat down and glanced at my watch. It was 7:10 p.m.: mere minutes to kickoff and counting.

"Still no Gordon," remarked Bill ominously.

"God damn it, he'd better get his ass here before game time," muttered Ed, obviously feeling the early twinges of a supernaturally generated jinxing.

Tod grinned as he finished reading an article in The Sporting News. "This writer," he said, not giving us the name, which was okay, because we hated most media clods anyway, "basically says New England might as well not even bother to take the field."

Suddenly, from out on the lawn, there arose such a clatter that half of us in the living room sprang to our feet to see what was the matter.

"It's Gordie and Julie!" announced Melody from the kitchen.

The noises we'd heard resulted from the Stinsons' squeaky old pickup reacting to frozen, unyielding ground as Gordon had pulled off the county road running past Joe and Suzanne's house and negotiated his way to one of the few remaining parking spaces on the snow-covered grass.

Somebody pushed open the front screen door — containing glass rather than screens, of course, during this time of year — and a few of us streamed out onto the wide porch, which was relatively free of snow and ice, thanks to a wooden overhang.

Lambeau and Lombardi, wearing their snug Packers coats, leaped from the bed of the truck and charged toward the house as Gordon and Julie climbed down from the cab. Luther and Sadie were barking excitedly somewhere indoors. Julie toted a cooler of beer, while Gordon balanced a steaming pan of bratwursts on each forearm. A Packers flag fluttered from a white plastic pole extending from the top of the truck's closed driver's window.

"'Bout time you're gettin' here!" yelled Ed.

"Game's over, Packers won!" I kidded.

"Ah, Christ," Gordon said, settling into a silence that seemed to indicate those two words were enough of an explanation of their tardiness to satisfy him, if no

74

one else.

"We got stopped by the police!" blurted Julie, her auburn curls bouncing against her neck as cans clinked together in her Isotoner grip.

"We didn't get stopped by the police," said Gordon, turning to glare at his wife as they approached the porch. A gust of wind, transporting flakes of snow like minuscule fighter pilots racing toward an enemy target, caused the aluminum foil covering the brats to rattle wickedly.

The Stinsons' Rottweilers were well ahead of them. They jumped onto the porch, completely ignoring the steps, and barreled inside the house to join the Mackeys' dogs in racing after one another.

"We were on Loretta Street over there," explained Gordon as he mounted the porch, jerking his head backward to indicate the direction from which he and Julie had come, "about a mile and a half, two miles away, and up in front of us I could see some cop cars blocking half the road, their lights flashing. They were stopping everybody who drove by."

"A sobriety checkpoint?" asked Tod.

Julie laughed. "That's what we thought at first, and there we were, both of us already fried to the gills. And there wasn't anywhere to turn around!"

"No," said Gordon, burping, "not a checkpoint. Turns out two guys broke into a house and tried to steal some jewelry. The owners were home, and they chased the would-be robbers away."

"They were on foot?"

Gordon nodded. "Their getaway car died on them. The cops were stopping motorists to ask them if they'd seen anybody fleeing through the neighborhood."

"Thank God for Lambeau and Lombardi," said Julie. "The officer who questioned us was so distracted by the dogs that I don't think he'd have noticed a meteor falling out of the sky, let alone that we'd had a few drinks too many."

"Fox just went to commercial!" bellowed Dave, who hadn't moved from his recliner in the living room. "Game's coming on!"

"Let's move!" cried Ed, leading us back into the warmth of the Mackey residence.

Joe had his entertainment center designed so that the TV sound issued from a pair of large, high-quality speakers mounted on opposite walls directly below the ceiling. Now he muted the commercial that was playing, raised a quieting hand, and declared, "All right, folks, here's the National Anthem!" He flipped some switches, activated a cassette tape in his nearby stereo system, and moments later the "Packerena" song blasted out at us.

"Hey, Packerena!" went the refrain, to everyone's delight.

"Hey, Packerena!" sang Yak Bak Devon.

Buster wandered into the room, sipping a Pabst Blue Ribbon and munching complacently on a dog biscuit as he danced a little jig.

Lombardi, the slightly larger of the pair of Rottweilers, barked his appreciation of the song while, I was certain, the dog's late namesake was smiling in his grave. In less than four hours, Vince would finally, after twenty-nine years of patient waiting, feel the peace that passeth all understanding upon the return of the trophy that bore his moniker to its rightful spot in Titletown, USA.

The moment of truth had arrived. The commercials and the "Packerena" song ended simultaneously, Joe unmuted the television, and Super Bowl XXXI began. John Madden was the color commentator, meaning there'd be a lot of chatter and bountiful usage of Xs and Os as he reviewed plays.

"Dogs!" called Suzanne from the kitchen. I heard the canines, including Lombardi, scramble toward her from various directions as she opened the side door and let them out to frolic in the snow.

The living room contingent went nuts when, on Green Bay's second play,

Brett Favre whipped a fifty-four-yard touchdown pass to Andre Rison on a deep post. The extra point drove home the point: the Pack intended to win. Roll commercials. I went out to the garage to get another beer. Darkness had fallen. Only a single dim bulb illuminated the garage. Meteorological conditions mated with the temperature inside the Coke machine to create thin threads of ice in my beverage the moment I opened it. I heard the dogs barking at one another out behind the garage. I strolled back into the house as beautiful Red Hot came out. I wanted to speak to her but instead chose to quickly return to the living room, arriving just as Doug Evans intercepted a Bledsoe pass. Later Chris Jacke kicked a field goal, making the score 10-0 in favor of the Pack.

A solid thump shook the front door, but nobody seemed to notice it except me. There were two more thumps, even more forceful. Obviously one or more of the dogs wanted back in. I opened the storm door and peered down through the lower glass pane of the outer door just as Luther rammed his head against the frame one last time. Strange behavior, I thought.

I opened the door, but instead of charging in, Luther backed away, staring wildly at me as he launched into an ear-splitting series of agitated barks.

"What's the matter, boy?" I asked. Boston terriers were nervous dogs, even in serene circumstances. Was Luther simply unable to control himself in this hectic party atmosphere?

Verbal dynamite in the form of assorted curses exploded in the living room as the Patriots made it into the end zone.

Luther kept barking, kept backing up. My inaction was upsetting him. But what did he want me to do? I stepped in his direction, and he immediately quit barking and dashed for the garage, which was out of sight around the corner of the house. I trotted after him, asking, "What's wrong, boy? Huh? What's wrong?"

When I entered the garage, I found out.

Two goons in Bears jackets stood next to the punch bowl, exactly where Angela and Lisa had been earlier. The goon on the left had an arm around Red Hot's throat, and his other hand held her right arm firmly. The goon on the right had a tight hold on Red Hot's left arm. The men didn't appear to have weapons, but they still failed to strike me as amiable members of my species, all things considered.

The reason they weren't moving was because Lambeau and Sadie, on opposite sides of the punch bowl, had them penned in. They were growling at Red Hot's assailants, the flesh around their mouths quivering, their whiskers twitching, their glistening teeth flashing in and out of view.

"Call of your dogs," snarled Goon Left. "We don't want to hurt anybody. We just need to put some distance between us and the cops. Too bad Little Red Riding Hood here had to come along as we were hot-wiring her Blazer."

"It was dark," whined Red Hot. "I didn't realize who they were or what they were doing until I got too close and they saw me and chased me in here."

"Shut up," Goon Left said to her. Then, to me: "She's got her keys, and we're taking her with us, in case we need a bargaining chip. Now get rid of these damned dogs, or I'll break her neck."

It didn't take a genius to figure out that these were the bungling jewelry thieves Gordon and Julie had mentioned.

Goon Right delivered a healthy sock to Red Hot's gut to punctuate his partner's statement about snapping her pretty, pale neck. She grunted and gurgled, although I think her padded vinyl jacket absorbed most of the blow. But the act of violence caused Lambeau, Sadie, and Luther to go absolutely ballistic. Both goons gripped her more securely than ever. Goon Right, nearest to Lambeau, could not take his eyes off the bloodthirsty, black-tongued Rottweiler.

"Don't hurt her!" I wailed, wondering at Lombardi's whereabouts. I heard a bunch of whining and moaning from inside the house, which had to mean either

New England had scored again or the Packers had done something moronic like fumble the ball.

I was missing the God-damned game! I had to do something, but I was aware that the dogs – none of them mine – wouldn't listen to me if I tried to call them off. Feeling a panic coming on, I bent down, picked up a dirty Wilson basketball, and held it in front of me. "You won't get away with this," I told the goons, wishing someone, anyone, had been present to back me up.

"What the hell you gonna do with that?" asked Goon Right with a mocking laugh as he gestured at the basketball.

Devoid of a game plan, I cocked my arm back and heaved the ball at his head as hard as I could. He easily ducked the orange sphere, which probably wouldn't have hit him anyway, and the ball bounced off the garage wall and came flying back at me. It smashed into my face, knocking me off my feet. The base of my skull collided with the hard cement floor of the garage.

"Oh, no!" cried Red Hot. "Mister, you okay?"

"What about these damned dogs?" screamed Goon Left, apparently to no one in particular.

I didn't lose consciousness, I didn't see stars or hear birds chirping, I didn't feel nauseous or dizzy — nothing along those lines. I felt fine, but I noticed a persistent clicking sound increasing in volume with every second. Was it a symptom of a concussion? Brain damage? The noise possessed a metallic quality.

I regained my feet just in time to see Lombardi, illuminated by a night light on the garage roof, jumping from one car hood to the next as he headed toward the garage. The clicking sounds were Lombardi's claws clattering against the vehicles' surfaces. He sprang off the car nearest to the garage and sailed in through the glassless window behind Red Hot and the goons as effortlessly as if he'd practiced the stunt a thousand times. He used his right front paw as a club, bringing it down against the back of Goon Left's head, and placed his left front paw squarely, almost delicately, between Red Hot's shoulder blades for balance. The momentum of the hundred-pound beast propelled him and the three interlocked humans forward, into the polar shallows of the punch bowl. Some of the drink splashed out onto Lambeau, Luther, and Sadie, who were sufficiently offended by this turn of events to leap into the bowl and join Lombardi in his attack upon the goons.

I gripped Red Hot (now Red Cold) underneath her arms and dragged her out of the drink as Stan and Dennis came into the garage for beers.

"What's going on?" asked Dennis.

"Patriots just scored again," grumbled Stan, as if dogs and people thrashing wildly in the punch bowl was nothing too unusual.

"Bears fans!" I shrieked, holding Red Hot in one arm while, using the other, I thrust an outstretched finger at the sorry, wet men fighting for their lives. "Fuckin' *Bears* fans!"

"Let's kill 'em!" roared Stan.

"Hell, yes!" concurred Dennis.

Naturally, though, they didn't end the lives of the hapless goons. But they did help me pull them out of the punch bowl, the dogs snapping at them all the way. While my friends tended to the goons, I took Red Hot inside, where she could get warm and dry before changing into some of Suzanne's clothes. Based on what Stan and Dennis told me later, all they did was beat the crap out of the foiled robbers, kicking them and punching them and stuff like that. This vigilante justice coincided perfectly with halftime — the Packers were leading 27-14 — so they didn't mind helping take care of the situation. Joe called the police, who came and arrested the goons.

After Red Hot had put herself together again oh so nicely, we traded introductions. She was single and had recently moved to this area from Wisconsin. An ardent Green Bay fan, she'd crashed the party after driving by and seeing Joe and Suzanne's plastic Packers helmet crowning their mailbox at the end of the driveway.

Red Hot thanked me for rescuing her. Humbly I said the dogs were more responsible for that than me. She sat on my lap to watch the second half of the game. The Packers scored some more points and won 35-21. Shortly afterward, back at my place in the company of Red Hot, I scored too.

Kent Robinson

This is the only piece of fiction I've ever written that might best be described as a romance. I don't read romance novels or stories and have no idea why I wrote this one. As a romance, it is probably more of a "genre" work than anything else in this book. Since it is one of my stories, I had to include it in a collection, so why not this one? It's certainly more at home here than in my upcoming volumes of horror, mystery and suspense, or science fiction and fantasy tales.

DOODLER IN LOVE

A few minutes ago I heard an expert, so-called, on one of those inane talk shows say that habitual doodlers doodle in an attempt to escape reality. I am stretched out on the living room couch, lights out, channel surfing, sighing, scratching repeatedly at the itch that pricks my neck whenever I get irritated, unsuccessfully trying to find a good black-and-white movie, or even a bad one, on TV. I love Walter Pidgeon and Deborah Kerr and especially Spencer Tracy. Heck, I love all those old stars. Some of the plots are dated, but that only makes the films more charming. At least the music back then took a back seat to the dialogue, where it belongs, and there weren't a hundred MTV-style visual cuts every sixty seconds. The actors stood still and looked at one another and engaged in actual conversation. Language seemed real, important. Characters weren't always leaping off the backs of trucks or shooting guns or diving for cover from endless explosions, although sometimes, of course, they did these things.

I think he called himself Dr. Barnard — the doodle expert, that is — but what difference does it make, really? He was instantly forgettable, like every expert on every talk show. Today my dog died. Just before that I bought a purple-colored scratcher at the corner gas station and won twenty thousand dollars. I managed to complete the X on the game in the right-hand corner. Then I went to the regional lottery office and picked up my check, and after that I went to my night class, where I ended up doodling in my spiral notebook for most of the three hours the session lasted.

Which reality am I desperate to flee, Dr. Barnard? The harsh reality of Luther's death? Or the happy reality of suddenly finding myself twenty grand richer? Well, okay, fourteen or so, since the government automatically gets to steal twenty-eight percent. Why would I or anyone want to dodge the latter reality? Sure, Big Brother ripped me off, but I still came out way ahead.

I am a doodler. Most "experts" are doodlers too, but they are full of doggy-doo. I do not doodle in doggy-doo fashion, meaning I do not go on television and doodle with the minds of the masses. My doodles are private, quiet, predominantly whimsical. My doodles hurt no one, send no aimless travelers down wrong roads. If I were ever given the opportunity to go on the tube and expound on anything — doodling included — would I take it? Nope.

An ex-boyfriend once told me I doodle because I am a dreamer. His name was Uwe, pronounced "OOH vay." He was Swedish, older than me, with big bones, freckled shoulders, and yellow hair. He said it as a compliment, with mist in his eyes, a bit of a daydreamer himself. He would always look over the tops of people's heads when he spoke to them. The truth is, I don't dream enough. I never have. I hold a demanding job, I do it well, and I never, ever call in sick, even when I am. Well, okay, once, when I had a severe case of the stomach flu. I've always had trouble letting my mind wander. Even at night, when I'm off work and relaxing, my mind doesn't really wander. I'm one for balancing the checkbook and putting fresh batteries in the smoke alarms and keeping my CDs in alphabetical order, going by the last name of the artist or the first word in the name of a group, excepting the word "the," of course. I am good at fulfilling my responsibilities both big and small. I tend not to do more than is expected of me as I see it, but I am skilled, if you will, at doing exactly what I think others should expect of me, which, sadly, in this age of defining everything down, often ends up being more than they wanted all along.

I have more than fifty notebooks of all sorts filled with doodles, and those are only the ones I've kept. I doodled for nearly ten years before I finally started saving them. I am now twenty-eight years old. I have never been married, but I think about marriage a lot. Where is my mind when I doodle? That's hard to say. Maybe my mind wanders more than I realize, but that doesn't mean I'm trying to *escape* from something, Dr. Barnard! When I doodle, is my mind on marriage? On the doodle itself? Regarding that last, it is, and it isn't. My mind, that is. On the doodle. Yet not. I sort of have to be paying attention to what I'm doing — or doodling — but on the other hand, sometimes I'll complete a doodle to my satisfaction and not recall any of the wrist or pencil movements or thought processes that spawned it.

My doodles are drawings of a sort, obviously, as all doodles are, but they are not artistic. They are not art. Even if all the world's art critics were to say they are, they aren't. Let me be clear about that. My doodles should not be in a museum someplace. Save museums for glass vessels filled with urine. I am not a miserable, luckless, undiscovered talent. I do not doodle out of some stupid repressed anger. No querulous victimization here. I will never be famous for my doodles, and that's okay, because I don't want to be. "Querulous": not a word you encounter very often, not a word most people can define. I had no idea what it meant either, until I came across it yesterday in the thesaurus while finishing a story for class.

Maybe I'd like to be a famous writer someday. Maybe that's why I'm taking the fiction-writing class three nights a week. Mondays, Wednesdays, and Thursdays. The truth is, I'm not exactly sure why I signed up for the class. Left to myself, I honestly don't think about fame that much. However, the writing instructor and some of my classmates seem obsessed with the subject to the point where they get me thinking and talking about it along with them. Whenever they drive me to the brink and I end up venting about becoming a famous writer, rather than simply *writing,* I usually spew something sarcastic or borderline bitter, like *Doesn't anybody just want to tell a good story?* or *Hemingway didn't care about fame,* even though I honestly have no idea whether he did or not, as I've never read anything about him and very little by him. Neither, apparently, have any of my classmates or the instructor, as nobody challenged my remark when I made it. Am I guilty of spreading disinformation about the late Ernest? Does the class see me as a genius, a well-read individual who is in the know concerning her dead authors? Does anyone care? Hello, is anyone out there? Maybe I should explode, literally explode, like dynamite does, rather than simply speak. Nobody listens to words anymore, and even fewer nobodies read them. To grab the attention, bodies must be mutilated! Buildings must be blown apart! Vehicles must crash! Maybe if I exploded I would have an impact. If I were a movie instead of a book, I'd hold the world in my spell.

Another doodler in class! A young man, very clean-shaven, who, as it so happens, is sitting as far away from me as possible: tonight, as on most nights, I'm at the last desk in the leftmost column, while my fellow doodler is seated at the front desk in the rightmost column. His name, if I recall correctly, is Craig. He has a low, shy voice that possesses a silky quality. When he speaks, his voice bleeds the tension from me, sucking it right out of my spine like soda up a straw. He is not bad looking: tall, dimple-faced, with a trim butt and nicely tanned forearms. I could easily get lost in my doodling around a soft, manly voice such as his. I am sure the movements of Craig's hand, as it holds the pen, are those of a doodler, not a note taker, especially when you factor in the faraway look in his eyes and the manner in which his head is propped in his free palm. No way is he paying attention to what the instructor is saying. The instructor, dressed in swirling, dark green tweeds that make him look like stacked spinach, is babbling on and on about how some janitor in Santa Ana just published his first novel, with movie rights going for half a million dollars. So what else is new? The *money* to be had by writers is the instructor's favorite theme. I wonder if he's paused to consider that the janitor had to *write* the damned book to begin with. I wonder if the instructor plans to have us read it or if he will analyze its merits, or lack thereof, for us. Is it well written? Poorly written? Does it matter? Only the money matters. Oh, yeah, and maybe getting published in the first place.

One of my most complex doodles, a highly pictorial one, is also a favorite of mine. I call him Mr. Happy Rain. I, myself, do not like rain, which is one reason I moved to southern California from Seattle soon after graduating from college. Mr. Happy Rain doesn't like precipitation either, but he <u>looks</u> like he does. I first doodled him into existence some five years ago, and since then I have doodled him from various angles and in various situations. He has a large nose, so large that it droops down between his legs and drags on the ground behind him as he walks. The trouble is, this makes his vast nostrils point skyward, so that when it rains they fill up with water, and he can't breathe through them. In such a circumstance, he is forced to open his mouth in order to get air, and when he does, the upturned corners of his lips are barely visible behind his huge schnozzle, and it looks like he's smiling. Thus his name.

I've rendered doodles of Mr. Happy Rain in a downpour, Mr. Happy Rain using his nostrils to play catch with a baseball, and Mr. Happy Rain dancing.

Craig is indeed a doodler. I introduce myself to him one night after class, and we leave the building together and walk to a nearby bar, where he shows me some of his doodles over drinks. They are sharp-edged, thickly lined, bursting with humor and anger. He likes doodling dynamite sticks and stairways and surprised faces with wickedly exaggerated features. He has eight years' worth of doodles in his apartment, he tells me. I am amazed and delighted to encounter another doodle hoarder. I show him a Mr. Happy Rain. He laughs in appreciation.

About class: he says he enjoyed my story "The Misfit," which I real aloud tonight. It's unnecessary for him to inform me of this, as I gathered from his remarks during class that he liked it. His kind comments were mainly what gave me the courage to speak to him afterward. He is scheduled to read his story next week, and I ask him if he's got it done. Almost, he says. What's it called? I pry. What's it about? He checks his watch and, as if answering, says, Let's go look at the dog. Not knowing what to expect, I follow him out of the bar and four blocks west, where we stop at a busy, brightly lit intersection and peer around the corner of a stucco building.

He glances at his watch once more and says any second now. Moments later a black dog appears at the mouth of the alley on the other side of the street. I feel a twinge of sorrow, thinking of my dear, departed Luther, who was a Rottweiler with crooked brown eyebrows and brown paws but otherwise black. The dog in the alley looks like a mutt.

Give him about a minute, says Craig. I do. After the time elapses, the mutt dashes across the street, to our side, and disappears into the continuing alley. Did you see him? asks Craig. I nod. He beams and says, Did you notice how none of the cars slowed down, honked, or swerved? Did you get a feeling the dog seemed invisible to motorists as it crossed the street? I confess I hadn't really thought about it, that I'm not always as observant as I should be. Nor, Craig adds, did the dog seem to pay any attention to the cars. I am getting sadder with each passing second, thinking about Luther. Every Monday, Wednesday, and Thursday, Craig explains, after class is dismissed and I've had a drink or two at the bar, I'll be walking by here, on my way home, at this exact time, and that dog appears at the mouth of the alley. And each time he goes running across the street, as if he's chasing something or someone, and disappears into the next length of alley. I've watched and watched, and I've never seen him return. Yet he's always back, at least three times a week, to repeat the process. So I decided to write a story about it. It's called "Dogged Dimension," it's science fiction, and in it the canine, who has the ability to travel between dimensions, protects our planet from an alien entity. The dog is the only creature who can see the alien, and the human narrator of my story is the only person who can see the dog. Why should that be? I ask. Well, that's because the narrator isn't really human; he is actually the malevolent alien, and he doesn't even realize it. He and the dog are from different dimensions, which in turn are separate from the human dimension. The dog and the alien can see Earth and its people, but we can't see them. The alien is a totally destructive creature with no sense of self or purpose and with no idea of what the dog is up to. The dog is a member of a race of benevolent beings who are intent on saving the Earth from the violent alien race. To the narrator, it appears as if the dog is dashing down an empty alley only because the dog hasn't yet managed to get in perfect sync with the alien's dimension. When the dog finally achieves dimensional synchronization at the end of the story, the narrator finds himself being attacked and eaten alive by the animal. Craig laughs. I know it's complicated and messed up, he says. He intends to work into the story an explanation of why dogs in real life frequently run out into the street: they're attempting to thwart alien aggressors bent on invading

Earth through dimensional portals.

I don't read much science fiction, I tell him. He voices concern over my suddenly watery eyes. I tell him about Luther, how he liked running out in the street after loud cars, which he found threatening. A Plymouth minus a muffler struck and killed him, I say. Craig puts his arm around me. He says he's sorry my dog died.

I accept Craig's invitation to go to his second-floor apartment, three blocks further west from where we've watched the dog. He owns hundreds of books, all alphabetized by the last names of the authors. Thinking of how my CDs are arranged, I tell him we have more than doodling in common.

He pops open a couple of beers for us. We sit next to each other, close, on his couch. I am comfortable with his closeness, and he, with mine. I don't know how I know this. I just do. The beer tastes good, and it's exactly the right temperature. He says he's glad to have met me and gives me a quick kiss on the mouth. I feel safe, somehow knowing this is as bold as he will get tonight. Good. Darn.

I am impressed by Craig's ability to observe a simple act of his reality — the running of the mutt down the alley — and write a story based on it. I tell him this. He tells me I can do it too, if I just take the time to use my imagination. I indicate this is easier said than done. He says not really.

I tell him how Luther walked with me down to the corner gas station. He sat outside while I went in and bought my winning lottery ticket. As I was coming back out, all smiles, the car with no muffler came barreling around the corner, and Luther ran out in front of it. He was squashed like a bug. The driver never stopped or slowed down. I didn't get a license plate number; the incident happened so fast, and I was frozen with fear and then grief as the scene unfolded before me.

There! exclaims Craig. There, you see, there's a story. Where? I ask. It's incredible, he says, you win twenty grand and lose your dog on the same day. Yes, that's true, I say. I thought about the mountain-and-valley emotional aspect of it myself. Well, he says, use those two seemingly unrelated occurrences to write a story that thematically explores whether it was worth it. Whether what was worth it? I ask. Whether it was worth twenty thousand dollars to lose your dog, he says. Connect the two events somehow. Maybe you could make it a time travel story: give your dog owner the opportunity to live that fateful day all over again, and give her the chance to save her dog by having her not purchase the lottery ticket.

I laugh and say I think I need to start reading science fiction. Maybe, I tell Craig, that will make my imagination as lively as his. We are sitting on the floor of the living room of my apartment. He laughs along with me, then picks up a note-book of my doodles on the nearby coffee table. He leafs through it and comments, not for the first time, on their artistic quality. I tell him, not for the first time, how flattered I am that he thinks so. He goes on and on about how they draw the eye in, the controlled lines, the way Mr. Happy Rain practically leaps off the page. He sees me blush. He leans over and kisses me long and full on the mouth. He does more. *We* do more. Good. Oh, yes, good! It feels great to be an artist. It feels great to be in love.

People are buying my doodles. They're buying them! I just sold a Mr. Happy Rain for five hundred dollars to a major Hollywood movie star who shall go un-named. I couldn't believe it! I couldn't believe that he wanted to meet me in person and that I actually got to talk to this, this, this *household name* for nearly fifteen minutes. Craig knows a gallery director in Santa Monica who agreed to display my doodles for three weeks. The second week is about over, and my doodles are attracting a lot of attention. I even got favorable reviews in the *Times* and the *L.*

A. Weekly. A little bit of fame and fortune don't seem so bad when they arrive almost by accident.

I've always thought Craig is quite the doodler too, but he says don't be silly, mine are a thousand times better. But Craig is much more serious than I am about the writing, which for me was just a passing fancy, I guess. In fact, while I've quit class and more or less abandoned the literary life, he has been plugging away on various manuscripts and recently sold "Dogged Dimension" to a science fiction magazine for ten dollars. I'd never seen him as happy as he was on the day when he got the acceptance letter — except, of course, on those frequent occasions when we get intimate with each other. Then he is very, *very* happy. And, needless to say, so am I.

Friends who know my literary tastes to any degree whatsoever know that my favorite novel of all time (so far anyway) is The World According to Garp *by John Irving. I laughed so hard while reading it that sometimes I was literally in tears. I'm sure Irving would be proud, as he has stated in interviews he considers himself a comic writer.*

One of the literary techniques Irving used in Garp *was foreshadowing, where certain events indicate or suggest that something else — usually unpleasant in nature — is to follow.*

I wanted to try my hand at foreshadowing too, so I wrote "Garrett Gosch Is Green." Though the story is filled with tragedy, it is meant to be funny. Humorless people call that sick. People with a sense of humor call that being able to perceive the comic in the tragic.

Believe it or not, "Garrett" was rejected forty-six times by as many different magazines before finally appearing in the short-lived publication (000) 000-0000. In all fairness to me, many of the editors who rejected the story told me they thought it was well-written and very funny. Most of the time, they said the story simply wasn't "right" for their magazines.

Stories not being "right" has been the main reason given for the rejection slips I've received over the years. I await the day when an editor comes along who accepts stories that are "wrong" for his magazine; I'll be able to market everything I write. Or right. You know what I mean.

GARRETT GOSCH IS GREEN

What set Garrett Gosch apart from other kids was his desire to be green.

No one — not even Garrett himself — could say for sure why the boy wanted to be green. Perhaps it was some quirk of heredity. Or perhaps the green-walled hospital in which he had been born had influenced him unduly.

When he was old enough to stand, Garrett would plant himself in front of the low dining-room window of his house and peer outside for hours at a stretch. What did he see?

Grass. *Green* grass. And beyond that, green trees!

Mrs. Gosch watched her son gaze out the window, day after day, until she finally said, "Well, I guess it won't hurt anything if you go out and play on the lawn for a while."

Her decision to take Garrett outside was not an easy one, for it forced her to confront the cause of her deepest fear.

It forced her to confront the nearby cypress swamp.

Mrs. Gosch's fear of the Tennessee swamp had started more than a decade earlier, after she had read a Frank Edwards paperback titled *Strange World,* which she had bought on a whim while browsing in the Munford, Tennessee, drugstore. Each of the brief tales in *Strange World* was supposedly true. Each dealt with a freakish incident that defied scientific explanation. The book had disturbed Mrs. Gosch a great deal. Her imagination gradually got the best of her. She began cringing at noises she heard coming from the swamp — noises that, before reading *Strange World,* she had never even noticed.

She became convinced that some sort of deadly creature lurked in the swamp and was responsible for the noises. She believed that someday she would have to defend herself and her family against the creature. So she drove to the nearest gun shop and purchased a Garand semiautomatic rifle, which she felt would be sufficient for killing the creature.

"Aw, there's nothin' out there," Stanley, her husband, told her repeatedly. "Nothin' at all to be scared of."

Once he was able to walk, Garrett liked to journey into the outer fringes of the swamp. He would search for gliders, the harmless turtles with the rounded chins. For pets, he would have preferred any of a number of other swamp denizens that sported more green than the sliders, but Mrs. Gosch didn't want frogs or snakes in the house.

Sometimes Garrett's best friend, Floyd Spradlin, would come over to play with him while the boys' mothers canned vegetables from the Gosches' huge garden. The women had met in church, where Mrs. Gosch would go to pray for safety from the swamp creature.

The boys invariably entered the swamp. They never went into the dark, vast interior of the swamp, however, where Floyd said they might get lost or commit the fatal mistake of stepping on a feisty, poisonous cottonmouth.

"My dad said he's seen cottonmouths longer than a pool cue," Floyd told Garrett as they hunted for sliders one day.

During another one of their trips into the outskirts of the swamp, Floyd asked Garrett, "You want to see the rest of the swamp?"

"I thought you were scared to go in further," said Garrett.

"We could see it from *above.*"

"You mean fly?"

Floyd nodded. "My dad has a plane."

Floyd had flown with his father at least a dozen times, and he described the experience to Garrett as seductively as he could.

A few days later, when Garrett and his dad were outside the house, the boy said, "Floyd and Mr. Spradlin want to take me flying."

It was obvious to Stanley that his son was excited about the prospect.

Suddenly Mrs. Gosch screamed from inside the house.

"Here we go again," remarked Stanley. "She thinks she's heard a monster."

Mrs. Gosch, carrying the Garand semiautomatic rifle, bolted outdoors and ran around to the north side of the house. Though they could not see her, Garrett and Stanley could hear her yelling at the peaceful swamp.

"Come out! Quit torturing my family!"

"You're torturing yourself," Stanley called out, guzzling a beer. When he drank, he became either antagonistic or apathetic. "Garrett and I aren't being tortured, 'cept by you."

"I saw it," came her reply. Obviously she was referring to the imagined creature. "It was short, like a hunchback or something."

"Right," muttered Stanley, burping magnificently. "Woman, you are full of fear."

"And you're drunk," she said, adopting a victorious tone of voice that implied she had exposed everything bad in her husband while disproving any of her own shortcomings.

Garrett was used to this type of exchange between his parents.

"Your fear is spreading like a cancer," said Stanley. "It's spread into the swamp, only there's nothing there for you to fear, 'cause this monster of yours doesn't exist. So you're frustrated, 'cause you've got to get that fear out of your system. Someday, woman, you're gonna go too far, and that fear will hurt somebody."

Angered by her husband's words, Mrs. Gosch stomped back into the house and refused to speak to Stanley for the rest of the day.

Garrett sometimes discussed greenness with his father.

"Not everyone in the world is the same color," he announced one day, as if he was the first person ever to notice this.

"But nobody is green," said Stanley.

Garrett brushed at his arms, as if to wipe away the color of his Caucasian skin. "It sure would be neat to be the first green person," he said.

"No it wouldn't," Stanley argued. "It would look ridiculous. Garrett, someday you're gonna have to forget about this green business. If you keep this up — always wearing green, always talking about green, always eating grass — your friends at school will start thinking you're weird."

Mrs. Gosch's sanity continued to deteriorate as a result of her fear of the unseen swamp creature. Her paranoia — combined with her increasingly ill feelings toward her husband — was turning her into a dangerous antisocial person. She had never fired the Garand semiautomatic rifle at Stanley — she was saving that for the creature. But she had flung her share of dishes at him.

One day Stanley arrived home earlier than usual in the old Ford pickup.

"You've quit another job, haven't you?" snarled Mrs. Gosch. Stanley's seeming inability to work steadily had been a source of aggravation to her for quite some time. "Two lousy weeks! Or did you get fired this time?"

"My boss was an asshole," said Stanley, climbing down out of the truck with a twelve-pack of beer under one arm. "I'll find something else before you know it."

Stanley was drinking beer more and more. His big belly drooped dramatically, making his skinny arms and legs look comical on such a bloated frame.

For drunken amusement, he had developed a game: after finishing a beer, he would stagger off the porch, turn and face the house, and fling the empty brown bottle over the roof to the other side. The object of the game was to toss the bottle into the bed of the rusty pickup truck, which was parked out front.

He had come close to hitting his wife once or twice.

97

When a bottle landed in the truck, it shattered loudly, scaring Mrs. Gosch almost as much as the swamp sounds did.

Even as Garrett was gearing up for his first opportunity to fly, Floyd visited him, bringing terrible news.

"We don't have a plane anymore," said Floyd. "Dad is going to buy some land, and he needed money, so he sold the plane."

Garrett had been so anxious to see, from above, the beautiful green swamp trees that stretched for miles, but vicious fate had robbed him of his chance. He had never felt so cheated in his entire life.

Denied that for which he longed the most — an incomparably satisfying green experience — Garrett no longer wished to associate with Floyd. He held him personally responsible for the ugly turn events had taken. When Floyd came over to the Gosch residence with his mother, Garrett would run into the swamp and hide.

Garrett trusted green far more than he trusted any person. Green had never betrayed him; he always felt good around green.

As Garrett grazed on the lawn one day, Floyd came pedaling toward the Gosch home on his bicycle.

"Let's go flying!" Floyd burst. "Dad bought a new plane!"

Garrett stood up slowly, wondering if he had heard correctly.

Floyd clumsily leapt off his bicycle, allowing it to flop over on its side. His blubbery body heaved with painful-sounding wheezes as he struggled to catch his breath.

"My dad — just got — a new plane," he gasped, "and tomorrow he's — taking us up!"

As Garrett observed the next day, the plane was not "new" in the sense that it had been recently built. Clearly Floyd had meant it was new to the Spradlin family.

"Climb in, boys!" called Mr. Spradlin, who was already in the cockpit.

Floyd let Garrett take the front seat, beside Mr. Spradlin, where he would have an excellent view of the trees below.

Mr. Spradlin played with his communications gear. Shortly he said, "Okay, boys, we're cleared for takeoff. Hang on to your hats!"

The plane sped down the runway, and within moments the Earth dropped out of Garrett's sight as the tiny vehicle left the ground, vibrating menacingly.

Soon the plane was flying over the swamp. Garrett leaned forward and looked down at the trees.

They were a sight more beautiful than any of Garrett's wildest green fantasies. The trees seemed to stretch on forever, even though Garrett knew the planet contained oceans and deserts and mountains and other boring geographical features.

Suddenly the engine coughed, and the plane lost altitude.

"What the hell — ?" blurted Mr. Spradlin.

The plane dipped violently to the right, slamming Floyd and Garrett against the cabin wall. Mr. Spradlin was able to level off the plane, and then he looked out the window.

The plane's left wing root had fractured. As Mr. Spradlin stared at the wing in horror, it tore loose from the fuselage and spun completely off the plane, plummeting into the swamp.

"We're going down!" he yelled. "Hang on to your hats!"

Mrs. Gosch had decided to turn in early. The stifling heat, combined with an inordinate amount of canning, had worn her out.

Occupying his usual position on the back porch, Stanley guzzled his sixth beer. Polishing it off, he wandered out into the back yard and threw the bottle over the roof, missing the truck completely.

Garrett and Floyd were tossed out of the plane as it crashed in the swamp. It leveled several bald cypress trees and was a total loss. Tiny fires burned throughout its length.

Garrett regained consciousness an hour after the crash. He lay motionless on his back in a shallow pool on the floor of the swamp. Eventually he found the courage to move. He propped himself up on his elbows, and pond water flowed down his neck from the hair at the back of his head.

When he stood up, he was pleased to discover that his only apparent injury was a mild throbbing in his right knee.

He felt heavier. Part of this was due to the water that had soaked into his clothes, but most of the gain in weight was a result of the long strands of Spanish moss that clung to him.

Staggering over to the demolished plane, Garrett knelt down next to some of the gently lapping flames and could see the lovely green strands of Spanish moss covering him.

Peering into the plane through a crack in the fuselage, he gasped when he saw the bloody, lifeless form of Mr. Spradlin. It was a queer sight: Mr. Spradlin had, in a fashion, hung onto his hat, but the head that still wore the baseball cap had been severed from its body and was half buried in mud, several feet away from the neck to which it had once been attached.

"Garrett, run!" cried Floyd.

Garrett made his way through the dark swamp, heading in the direction from which Floyd's voice had issued.

"Garrett, there's cottonmouths!"

Garrett moved close enough to Floyd to see that his friend's blubbery frame was covered with slippery cottonmouth snakes. At least a dozen of them slithered over Floyd's body, some more than six feet long.

"I'm a goner, Garrett! Run!"

Mrs. Gosch tossed and turned in bed. In spite of her weariness, she was unable to sleep. She lay listening to every sound that issued from the swamp.

Tonight, she thought, I will kill that damned swamp creature.

She got out of bed and tiptoed to the living room, where she picked up the rifle and sat in the chair next to the screen door. She remained there, listening to the swamp, the rifle crosswise in her lap.

As she was about to fall asleep in the chair, she heard it: the deadly, stealthy swamp creature, treading nearby. It sounded more determined than ever, which convinced Mrs. Gosch that tonight was when the creature would actually attack.

She dashed out the door, brandishing the rifle. As she stared at the edge of the swamp, a dwarfish humanoid shape popped out onto the lawn.

She aimed the gun and pulled the trigger as the shape yelled, "Mom!"

The bullet ripped through the Spanish moss and pierced Garrett's brain, killing him instantly.

Stanley heard the gun go off the moment he threw his ninth beer bottle over the roof of the house. He was quite drunk by then, and bottles were flying everywhere.

The ninth bottle smashed against Mrs. Gosch's head, fracturing her skull and killing her instantly too.

The sound of the rifle being fired was a real shock to Stanley; it was the first time his wife had ever gone this far.

He ran around to the north side of the house. His drunken haze quickly dissipated as he surveyed the scene before him. He didn't know why Garrett had been goofing off at the edge of the swamp when he should have been flying, but it was clear Mrs. Gosch had shot him. Stanley then figured out that the beer bottle had caused his wife's death.

He called the police. They came to the Gosch home and made a report. Stanley was arrested for involuntary manslaughter. Before he could go to trial, he died of cirrhosis of the liver — not in as instant a fashion as his wife and son.

The Tennessee cypress swamp remained, as always, filled with greenness.

Another story, along with "A Death Sentence," about suicide, this one concerning a truly disturbed man who begins writing notes....

SUICIDE NOT

Dear World:

I have made up my mind, once and for all, to kill myself. If you're reading this note, you'll realize I've gone ahead with the deed.

One philosophy holds that suicide is a selfish, irresponsible act, bringing untold pain down upon friends and family members. That is one of the most ridiculous things I've ever heard. If the survivors harbor that attitude, imagine how selfish they must be, to ignore the desperation and misery that drove one so close to them to end his or her life. Would a person commit suicide for selfish reasons, given that he or she would not be around to relish the fruits of such conceited behavior? All those canards about selfishness are terribly misleading. On the contrary, suicide is perfectly selfless.

In any event, I seem to be straying from the specific subject at hand — namely, my impending death. I would like to outline the shape my existence has taken, such that I am compelled to terminate it.

It's all about rejection, I tell you. Rejection is a terrible thing, and I have suffered because of it far more than any man should.

First there was the wife, Nancy, who no longer holds that position. I don't mean to make it sound like a job. That is, Nancy was not a slave around the apartment, though she insisted that was my attitude toward her. She loved to wield that crutch in order to get her way. She

Let me start again.

For a while I loved her, and she loved me. That's usually the way it goes. I didn't mind that she held a job, that she sometimes earned more in a week than I did in a month (two hundred dollars more in the most extreme case, not that I cared or paid much attention). We split up the household duties. Then again, I was, I am, a man, which carries with it certain requirements, certain tasks that must of necessity be avoided

Oh, hell, that's not it; that's not it at all. I've lost track of the point here. I'm too depressed to continue. Too drunk. Too tired.

Dear World:

In between sentences I stare at the vial of cyanide, which, coincidentally enough, is sitting right beside the typewriter. After all, it's the typewriter that has driven me to this point.

The only reason you're reading this note is because I've finally decided to drink the poison and end it all. Don't think you're somehow superior for "toughing it out," because my decision clearly indicates a heightened degree of intellectual behavior. I planned it this way, down to the most minute detail. I'm talking to you. I knew I would kill myself immediately after finishing this note, that you would be the one to read these words. If only you possessed as much control over your destiny. You're just another blind, simple creature who's decided to plod along through life for a little while longer; there's nothing noble about that, and don't you forget it.

Rejection is the reason for my demise. Nancy married me purely out of misguided selfishness. I see that now. But when she didn't have that Porsche by the time she was thirty, thanks to her deadbeat husband, she decided to hit the road and

Obviously I can't continue in this tone, because you're liable to be a woman cop. Okay, so maybe I don't exactly know who will be the one to read these harrowing words, sometimes I get carried away. Nevertheless, police lady, what would you do if you found this note next to my rigid body? After reading it would you turn it in as evidence, hoping it could make the news and thereby serve as a lesson to another man who might one day find himself locked into the same bitter circumstances as those from which I suffered? Or would you tear it up and stuff it in your pocket to keep its gripping insights, its ugly truths, hidden from society? I think the latter would pertain, but I'm not about to give you the opportunity to make a choice. No one, least of all you, will ever lay eyes upon these comments. In fact, I'm going to yank the paper out of the typewriter, crumple it up, and toss it in the wastebasket.

So *there!*

Dear Mr. President:

Before you receive this note, I will have killed myself in a most undramatic fashion, that being the proper fate for an undramatic man such as me.

You may not even get this letter, being leader of a nation while I am but an insignificant member of the nonvoting electorate. Probably some low-level secretary will open the envelope, gaze dumbly at my statements, and ultimately toss the note aside, not wishing to bother the chief executive with the disturbing contents.

I did not vote for you, because I do not care. Do not flatter your life's work by assuming I simply don't care for you personally, for it is politics in general I dislike. I resent having to formulate my ideas of my future within your, or anyone else's, political framework, be it communism or socialism or democracy. I don't even like the names themselves, as they inevitably boil down to some mode of living that robs me of my freedoms and gives me no choice but to compromise. I resent politics, I resent concepts, I resent sharing this planet with other human beings whose beliefs are different than mine. Not only do I resent them, but I reject them too. I am familiar company with rejection: I've been intimate with it my entire life.

Just between you and me, I don't really see where people are any freer in a democracy than they are, say, under a dictator. As far as I can determine, it's always the evil against the innocent, the string pullers against the puppets, the rich against the poor.

And then there's this law against committing suicide. Now why should you or anyone else in political office — or even my next-door neighbor, for that matter — care whether a lowlife like me kills myself? The fact is, you don't care. So why the hypocrisy? I could unsuccessfully attempt to off myself and afterward undergo incarceration, thanks to your stupid law. Let's face it, suicide is a victimless crime, relieving the deceased of his misery and causing agony only among the selfish survivors who, because of their selfishness, fully deserve their so-called pain. Here again we are talking about hypocrisy, a crippling problem that runs rampant throughout this nation, that no one in a post such as yours ever bothers to recognize, precisely because you use it for your own purposes. Hypocrisy. It's a far more insidious ill than murder, drug abuse, or theft. What I could tell you — but never mind, never mind, I didn't write you this note in order to get involved in a debate of such serious magnitude, so let's just drop it.

To continue on the subject of suicide and its illegality: Do you expect the populace to obey the law when it falls below a respectable level as it has here in the remaining years of the twentieth century? More and more, people thumb their noses at the law, and so they should. God damn it, now we, the common folk, are forced by our government to bail out the savings and loan industry, simply because there are, in that fiasco, too many white-collar crooks to round up. Why bother to hunt them down and arrest them when you can easily heap another burden on the backs of the middle class? I read that rescue efforts in this matter will cost each

American household more than five thousand dollars. I can't even afford to pay my alimony, let alone part with an entire five grand. And that doesn't begin to address the fact that I wouldn't *want* to do it even if I could afford it.

But again I ramble. The truth is, I've been rambling a lot lately, I sit down at the typewriter with no hope, no inspiration, sometimes I'm not even aware of what keys my fingers are striking. Other times there's nothing but the blank page that I eventually fill with words thanks mainly to an eruption of physical energy fueled by an enormous amount of alcohol. I begin banging the keys, clattering out words of utter wretchedness, You will reject me, as the editors and publishers and wife and parents have done. Rejection feeds on me, feeds off my soul, though if there's one thing I won't do it's try to come off as some sort of martyr. I've had an enjoyable life in many respects — always healthy, ever able to laugh even when faced with the darkest circumstances, laid regularly, at least in my younger years, by a stunning array of good-looking women who thought I was handsome or intriguing or who knows what, who knows, who gives a shit, the point is, the point is, a roll in the hay is a roll in the hay, if you know what I mean

To Whom It May Concern:

This note, I swear to God, will be the last I ever write. I am going to kill myself. There may be a lot of things I cannot do, but if there's one thing I can carry out with ease, it's suicide. Who better to commit suicide than oneself? A little joke there, a little humor. Suicide is one aspect of life over which each person has total control. That's why it's a crime: the very idea of the average citizen, a nobody as far as society's power structure is concerned, wrenching control from the political lords of the moment, shaking a fist at the sky, and yelling that this is *my* life, *my* fate, get out of the way, don't try to stop me from killing myself, you legislating assholes, I've had just about all I can take. I can take. I am in control for once. In control. Yes. I am. In. Control.

Dear Mother:

Once again, if I must say it, it's rejection that has ruined my existence. Not presidents, not women — who, if anything, have been largely accepting, the main exception being the wife — not the law, or my own financial mismanagement. These seem to be neither caring nor cruel but rather oddly disinterested.

"Dear Mother"? Why do I even bother? Have I lost so much dignity as to write a suicide note to my own mother? I thought I was more of a man than that, but then, I am my mother's son.

I know you don't care, so never mind.

By the way, does Dad ever come by to beat you up for old time's sake? I hope so. Considering what you helped my life to become, I figure you deserve it.

Dear Dr. Loplis:

Enclosed is a check for you final bill. To pay you, I had to take out another loan from the credit union. The loan official insisted it would be my last. But what do you care? I'm merely something you can discuss with your fellow psychiatrists over lunch or, at best, someone you occasionally sympathize with in your more altruistic moments.

I said "final bill." That's because I don't wish to see you anymore. I hired you — though now I'm not sure why — and I can fire you.

Dear Diary:

Today I received five rejection slips in the mail. The rejected material was some of my best and most recent writing.

Curiously, I was overcome by a warm, safe feeling that still lingers.

Dear Diary:

Why have I been writing diary entries? I don't even keep a diary. This is a typewriter, for Christ's sake.

Dear Death:

You will not take me. Surprised? Well, I will not succumb to you. I'm sorry to disappoint you, but that's the way it is.

Yes, I am sorry, for you are what I once wanted, as much as you still want me. I was ready for you, or so I thought. I was sick and tired of the rejected manuscripts, the annoying phone calls from lawyers representing the thing that was once my wife, political leaders who have self-interest in mind more than the future of the republic of which I am, grudgingly, a part.

But suicide is, unfortunately, out of the question. The vial of cyanide is sitting right here, an arm's length away. Suicide, cyanide, joy ride. All I would need to do is reach out, grab the vial, snap off the top, and drink the contents.

However, I cannot.

Acceptance of any kind is intolerable. I have become a friend of rejection, a companion, I now recognize it as an integral component of the entity that is me — not by choice, you understand, and certainly not in any quick fashion, but nevertheless, nevertheless, here I am. The point is, I don't like the situation any more than you do. But ask yourself this: Having grown accustomed to a seeming eternity of rejection, how can I ever give myself up to your cold, accepting embrace, Death? Acceptance is — must be regarded as — a terrible monster. I cannot face it. I fear your icy grasp, because in surrendering to it, I surrender to acceptance. To enter into your fold, to be whisked away to some dark region that would have me — it's all too much, too much, and my heart pounds dangerously in even pondering the possibility.

I'm going to get up from my desk, flush the cyanide down the toilet, and return here to my desk to start writing that novel I've been putting off. Suddenly I am dying to get to it. Ha, ha, another little joke there, Death. *Death. Dying* to get to it. It's life that I love, life that rejects me. No more feeble suicide notes. No more self-pitying prattle. Who knows, perhaps I'll give up the booze as well, though there is something to be said for keeping self-imposed demands within a realistic framework, for taking one day at a time, as it were.

I'm very proud of this story if for no other reason than that its publication in Zeta Magazine *earned me my first handsome paycheck for a work of fiction. Hey, I believe in capitalism. A free, competitive market motivated by profit is what runs this nation, and without it, the United States would be a shithole, just like so many non-capitalistic countries in the world.*

THE GOOD PARENTS OF BILLY BAXTER

Finally the day arrived when Billy Baxter succeeded in raiding the kitchen wastebasket.

That morning, as on many mornings, he watched his father remove the mysterious vial of cloudy gray liquid from the refrigerator door's top shelf. Then Mr. Baxter swung around and, from the cupboard opposite the Kelvinator, pulled out the tiny alcohol pad and the thin cylindrical object with the orange cap — a syringe, as Mr. Baxter had called it on one occasion, when he yelled into the adjoining room to tell Billy's mother that it wasn't working right, that it was the third dud from the same box, that a refund from the pharmacy was definitely in order.

Seven-year-old Billy had never forgotten that word *syringe.* Twice he had asked Mr. Baxter what a syringe was for, but both times he only got his face slapped for not minding his own business. So he had stopped asking. But the punishment he had received as a result of his inquiries kept the word lodged firmly in his memory.

Billy, no less curious about life than most children, wanted to know more about syringes. Unlike his father, Billy didn't get to use them, and he wondered why.

Before eating breakfast, Mr. Baxter would jab the needle into his arm or stomach — rubbing the alcohol pad against the target before and after — and then he would throw the syringe and pad into the wastebasket beneath the kitchen sink.

Billy had sometimes attempted to sift through the contents of the wastebasket in search of a discarded syringe, but his mother invariably caught and spanked him.

"Bad boy!" she would screech, yanking on his little arm so violently that sometimes it was sore for days afterward. She would lower her wrinkled, angry face down next to his, her sour breath burning its way into his nostrils. "You know better than to rummage through trash." And she would hit him some more, never stopping until he yelled in pain or cried.

Billy might have better understood syringes if his parents — like most parents with children who were Billy's age — had taken him to the family doctor to be vaccinated against tuberculosis and measles and other diseases. After all, Billy had already completed first grade, and a state law declared that children in the public schools were to obtain the proper vaccinations before enrolling as elementary students. But with a handful of falsified medical documents, backed by lies told to the school nurse, Billy's parents had managed to get their son into school without his ever having received a single injection.

Billy's parents had no qualms about lying to the school nurse, because they felt they were ultimately carrying out God's will. They had begun to see the school corporation as evil.

A friend of the Baxters, who belonged to the same church and many of the same civic and community organizations that they did, had a daughter who attended junior high school. During a PTA meeting at the daughter's school, this friend — the girl's mother — had chanced upon a copy of *Hamlet* on a shelf in the library. The mother had recently participated in a public burning of copies of this play at another school corporation, and she was not about to let her own daughter be subjected to material that she had been told was foul and sinful in the extreme — material that, incidentally, she had never read herself. So she had stuffed the book in her purse, taken it home, and thrown it in the garbage can.

"Good for you!" Mrs. Baxter had cheered when the mother related her story, and Mr. Baxter had applauded enthusiastically.

Later, because of the story told by the daughter's mother, Billy's parents gave serious consideration to switching their son from the public school corporation to a private one. *Hamlet* indeed!

Even if they didn't pull Billy out, his parents certainly weren't going to allow public school officials to tell them when to take their son to the doctor.

Mr. Baxter, who always seemed to Billy as if he were behind in doing the things he had to do, didn't like it when his son asked him questions. He made time for Billy when there weren't more pressing matters to deal with.

Billy's mother was more accessible to him than his father, but when the end of the month rolled around and she began writing checks to pay the bills, she didn't want to be bothered by him either.

Late one morning Billy forgot to leave his mother alone as she wrote out the checks. He posed a question to her.

"When are we going to eat?"

"Go play!" snarled Mrs. Baxter, looking up from the check ledger and glaring at Billy as she pointed outside.

His last full meal had been yesterday's lunch. He was starving. Billy could clearly remember when the three of them had regularly sat down together for two big meals a day, but they hadn't done that in a long time.

"I'm too tired to play," argued Billy. "I'm hungry."

"Now see here, young man — " Mrs. Baxter leapt out of her chair and, with the palm of her hand, smacked Billy once on the buttocks, hard, sending his frail frame lurching wildly toward the door leading to the back yard. Normally she would have hit him some more, but instead she quickly resumed her seat, expunging Billy from her thoughts, preoccupied solely with the checks.

Billy had no way of knowing that his parents didn't have as much money available for food as they once had. They had decided to put more of their money into what they regarded as a good cause by mailing lots of it to three of their favorite TV evangelists.

Sometimes Billy's parents made him watch the evangelists' stupid programs along with them. The shows bored Billy to death. He much preferred *The Flintstones* or *The Incredible Hulk*.

"Where is that irresponsible babysitter?" asked the frustrated Mrs. Baxter.

Billy went into the living room and began idly playing with his toy trucks. he sensed his mother's growing impatience. He knew his parents were anxious to get to another one of the many community meetings they attended.

I don't need a babysitter, thought Billy. I'm not a baby.

But he couldn't tell his parents that; they would have to conceive of the idea without his prompting. If he tried to tell them he was old enough to stay home by himself, not only would he get spanked for being insolent, they would end up dragging him along with them to their meeting, which he knew from experience would be almost as bad as having to listen to the TV evangelists.

"Dear," Mr. Baxter said to his wife, "we can't wait much longer. We've got to stop at the drugstore so that I can buy some insulin. I'm out, you know."

Billy perked up at the sound of the new word: *insulin*. What was insulin? Billy suddenly found himself wanting to know, but he was not about to ask Mr. Baxter.

"Billy, come here," called Mrs. Baxter.

Billy got up off the floor and entered his parents' bedroom, where his mother and father took turns surveying themselves in the mirror, making sure they were dressed properly.

Mrs. Baxter knelt down beside Billy and ran her fingers through his hair. "We've got to leave," she told him, "but there's no babysitter."

Billy didn't know how he was supposed to respond to that statement, so he said nothing.

"If we leave you home by yourself," said Mr. Baxter, adjusting his necktie, "will you be okay? You won't be scared, will you?"

Oh boy! thought Billy, standing very still and trying not to look excited. They're really going to do it; they're going to let me stay home by myself. He remained silent, trying to imagine what it would be like.

Mrs. Baxter misinterpreted Billy's speechlessness as fear. She looked up at her husband and said, "Well, perhaps we should take him with us — "

"No, no," said Mr. Baxter, shaking his head. "Not this time. Too many liberals will be there tonight, shooting off at the mouth. I don't want them polluting Billy's mind. The last thing this world needs is another abortion clinic."

"But he's only seven years old, and he's never stayed by himself before, and — "

"I'm not afraid," Billy informed his mother. "I don't need a babysitter. I'm big enough."

"That's right," agreed Mr. Baxter in an assuring tone. "He's a big boy. Before you know it, he'll be a man, out on his own. Just think — eight years old in June."

"July," Billy said.

"What?"

"My birthday is in July, not June."

For correcting his father, Billy got his face slapped. The hand came down from the side, swiftly and unexpectedly, and the force of the blow knocked him backward. Billy stood staring at his father, wondering how he could go from being so nice to so mean so suddenly.

By the time his parents left for the meeting at the town hall, the red splotches on Billy's face, where Mr. Baxter had slapped him, had disappeared.

Billy's memory of the incident had all but disappeared as well, at least for now. He was too excited over having the whole house to himself — even if only for a couple of hours — to think about anything else.

With Mrs. Baxter out of the kitchen, he could search for things to eat without having to look over his shoulder every few seconds. Once he fed himself, maybe his stomach would stop growling.

But even before he satisfied his hunger, he had to retrieve the syringe from the wastebasket. Mrs. Baxter hadn't emptied the trash all day, so Billy knew the syringe from that morning was still there.

Billy dumped half the contents of the wastebasket out onto the floor before the syringe at last came tumbling out, landing between his legs. He picked it up and eyed it closely. Mr. Baxter hadn't pulled the needle out after using the syringe, as the family doctor had recommended. His dad never did that.

Billy examined the needle. It was short, only half an inch long, and it didn't frighten him. After all, he was staying home alone these days. Nothing was supposed to scare you once you were allowed to stay home by yourself.

Billy dragged a chair over to the refrigerator, opening the door of the appliance. Standing on the seat of the chair, he inspected the top shelf of the refrigerator door. It was completely empty, except for a small jar of olives.

Where was the vial of gray liquid? Mr. Baxter pulled it off the top shelf every morning. Billy was certain.

Then Billy remembered what he had overheard his father saying earlier in the evening — about being out of something called insulin. Maybe insulin was what they gray, watery stuff was called. Maybe you needed insulin to make the syringe work correctly.

Climbing down off the chair and closing the refrigerator door, Billy returned to the wastebasket, picking his way carefully through the pieces of refuse he hadn't already scattered across the kitchen floor. Methodically he searched for the discarded insulin container.

And there it was!

Billy held the vial up to the light. A vertical gap in the label revealed some insulin still in the vial.

It's not all gone, thought Billy. There's still some in there I can use.

After scaling the chair to grab an alcohol pad out of the cupboard, Billy sat back down on the floor and rolled the insulin vial between his hands, as he had seen his father do. Then he dashed the alcohol pad across the top of the vial and, pulling back the plunger of the syringe, inserted the needle into the vial, pushing the plunger down.

Billy inverted the vial above the syringe and began to pull the plunger out again. It was difficult to coordinate this movement, and Billy dropped the vial and syringe three times before he managed to pull the plunger all the way out to the end of the syringe. Then he removed the needle from the vial and examined the syringe's interior.

The insulin was now inside the syringe, filling it a little less than a fourth of the way. Billy was ecstatic. He felt as if he had performed a magic trick of some sort.

Billy didn't know — nor would he have cared if he had known — that most of the syringe was filled merely with air.

The rest is easy, he thought.

Removing his shirt, Billy lifted the alcohol pad off the dirty floor and rubbed it against his belly, a few inches to the left of, and slightly above, his navel, as his father sometimes did. Then he grabbed the syringe and pointed the needle at the wet spot on his skin.

After an instant's hesitation, he jabbed the needle into the wet spot. There was a slight burning sensation that caused Billy's breath to catch, but there was no pain to speak of, really.

Taking the final step, Billy pushed the plunger back down to the other end of the syringe.

The resulting aneurysm — the rupturing of the vital blood vessel, caused by the air in the syringe — killed Billy, painfully and almost instantly.

In spite of his parents, Billy had found out about syringes.

Yes, I can't deny the charge, this is a story — albeit a funny one, I hope — about farting. We all do it, so why not explore the subject in fiction?

I make no apologies for this or any story I've written or might someday write. The transformation of ideas into stories is the only important thing, and it crowds out all else, unable to be resisted. To paraphrase a lyric by my favorite rock-'n'-roll musician, Joe Walsh, in his "The Radio Song," the story helps me write itself down.

Coming soon: a funny story by me about puking. Just kidding!

FLATUS

This time it's the butler's revenge that escapes, with nary a squeak nor hiss, as he makes love. He hopes it will not stink or, leastways, that the stench will not linger, but his latest gaseous discharge proves to be a dawdling nose closer, as usual.

"God," the woman beneath him moans, relinquishing her grasp on his bulging biceps and waving a hand in the vicinity of her nose. "That horrible smell. The very essence of decay. Are your pants on fire?"

"Well," mutters the embarrassed Ralph, "in a manner of speaking, yes," and even though his slacks lie with the rest of his attire, and hers, in a heap at the foot of the bed — and she is completely aware of this — he admits to himself that one of his more private areas normally covered by that item of clothing is definitely, in a figurative sense, ablaze. "You see, I have this problem of being unable to stop the release of intestinal gas when procreating. My own personal species of bacterial infection seems synchronized with orgasm such that — "

"Oh, I don't want to hear it," the blonde declares, pushing him off of her and clambering to her feet, and Ralph does not doubt his latest bar pickup's statement.

After all, the subject of uncontrollable farting is not exactly appealing during intimate moments like this, if ever, and besides, he has never before attempted to explain his problem to any woman with whom he has shared carnal pleasures. He realizes how ridiculous he must sound and feels like even more of a fool for attempting to say anything in his own defense.

But he is fed up with his flatulence. It is an affliction that is both unprecedented and unfair — breaking wind at each climax, without fail. Medical science has thus far failed to provide him with an explanation or solution, and in the meantime his romantic life continues to deteriorate. Seldom are the women he is with able to come themselves, because their peak moments are inevitably interrupted by the farts, the maddeningly ill-timed and unstoppable farts.

"Whew!" she blurts, her facial features caving in, crumpling against themselves in an expression of disgust as she dresses in hasty, jerky motions. "Jesus, that ought to be outlawed."

"Give me a break," he finally says, irritated by her uncompromising attitude. "I farted; I cut the cheese. It's not as if I killed somebody or committed blasphemy. Don't make a mountain out of a fucking molehill. After all, you seemed to be enjoying yourself up to a certain point, so don't blow this all out of proportion."

She sneers at him.

"PFOOOOOOT!" explodes Ralph's anus, and he forces this second volcanic eruption purely out of spite. "I did that one on purpose," he informs her. "BUUUURRRROOOOOOM!" his butt bellows, filling the room with fetor, his sphincter muscles taking over for those in his jaws. After all, some response to the woman is essential, yet it is hopeless to try to reason with her. Words mean less than rectal gusts, which themselves represent nothing except his own dismissal of her. She is offended beyond repair, she already has ideas of better ways to spend the remainder of the night, so screw it, screw her, what can he possibly do, what can he say, to repair matters? Nothing, of course, as usual.

She slips through the doorway, vanishing into a dense interplay of shadows. He gives her the finger and proclaims, "BRRRRRRRUUUUM!" Alone and mildly inebriated, he closes his eyes in the oppressive, noiseless solitude of his apartment. The immobilizing, odoriferous weight he is so used to presses against him from all sides, pinning him to the mattress, and eventually he falls asleep.

"Doctor," he says, "while I am aware my problem seems humorous on the surface, you can't imagine how destructive it is to my social life. The last thing women want to be subjected to as they engage in sex is the repulsive aroma of a fart. The loud ones are the worst, rudely calling out their existence to any whose olfactory nerves might be ineffectual, but even the silent ones are usually ghastly, smelling as awful as they do. Always there is the smell, the horrible smell — "

"Beer," interjects the doctor, trying to be of some help, but Ralph easily sees that it is all the man can do to choke back his laughter, "beer is known to produce intestinal gas in the stomachs or bowels of many individuals, and you earlier stated that you meet the majority of your women in bars. Perhaps you should consider switching to a wine cooler or abandoning the habit of drinking altogether."

Wine cooler. For God's sake, thinks Ralph, is that the best this quack can do? Ralph hates doctors, has always hated them, and this guy is no exception. None of them has ever put forward any realistic hope of treating his condition, and the lame suggestions they do manage to proffer are courses of action he has long since taken and abandoned. For lengthy periods he has tried drinking only orange juice or other beverages or combinations thereof; giving up drinking totally; removing certain foods from his diet or adding others; engaging in various exercises; administering enemas; inserting suppositories; consuming packages of Rolaids; praying; and writing letters of apology to people he may have wronged in the past, no matter how long ago. But nothing has worked. Everything has proven to be useless. And he is utterly sick and tired of going to one money-grubbing doctor after another and hearing the same bland recommendations over and over. "You sons of bitches," he says, "you're all alike, you take my weight and blood pressure, ram a Popsickle stick down my throat, and then tell me absolutely nothing of value. All you want is my money. Seventy-five dollars for a ten-minute office visit. It's an outrage. Just what have you done here this morning to earn my seventy-five dollars? Do you realize how severe my problem is? Have you put yourself in my place even for a second? Imagine being unable to provide women with an orgiastic thrill because of unrestrainable farting. My reputation for breaking wind is starting to get around, it's not as easy as it once was for me to find a one-night stand. It's not fair, I tell you. This isn't a joke, you understand, this is a painful issue I — "

"You're babbling," says the doctor, clearly upset by Ralph's attacks on his character and his profession. "I think perhaps your, ah, problem may be psychosomatic in nature and that you need to consult — "

"Oh, no," declares Ralph as he leaps off the examination table in the tiny cubicle, "I'm not about to visit a God-damned shrink. I have even less respect for psychiatry than I do for modern medicine. Doctor, I can see we're getting nowhere here, that we are wasting each other's time, so I'm leaving, I'm going back to work. I'll cope with my unfortunate and admittedly peculiar circumstances, but you can forget the crazy idea that I'll ever end up on some analyst's couch, because I won't."

"Tell me about your childhood," says Dr. Roper, fidgeting with her glasses, and Ralph suspects he couldn't have picked a more unsuitable, exasperating psychiatrist (not that any nut doctor could benefit him; the futility of this session is a

122

foregone conclusion as far as he is concerned); the timbre of her voice, her nervous fussing, the strategically bright clothing hanging from her tall, trim frame like elemental, threaded therapy — it's all more than he can take. He hasn't been on the couch for even a full minute, and already he is disgusted and infuriated. He should have expected the worst when he was able to immediately arrange a session with this woman by simply walking in off the street. More and more he finds himself engaging in the habit of walking, of dragging himself from one bar to the next, and after drinking his lunch today he decided to write off the afternoon's work and go see a deficiency expert for a good laugh.

But he is not laughing. Nothing is funny. He feels only the familiar rage and cynicism. "My childhood," he mutters. "You aren't even aware of what I'm suffering from, but already you are curious about my childhood. What is it with you shrinks and childhood?"

"Sir," Dr. Roper says, a hand moving from her glasses down to her scarf, "you don't need to get so upset, I'm only trying to get to the root of your problem."

"The problem," ralph informs her, "is that I can't screw without farting. Over the years I must have banged at least two hundred women — that's no lie, I'm not exaggerating here, believe me — but always the instant of ejaculation is accompanied by at least one huge, reeking fart. Imagine that you and I are naked and entangled — "

"Now listen here — "

" — we're in bed or perhaps on top of a pool table, wherever, our breathing is heavy, our heartbeats race, we're sweating, those long legs of yours are tight around my waist, your eyes are closed and your mouth open as you moan while I thrust myself repeatedly into you — "

"I beg your pardon!"

" — and as you find yourself approaching orgasm, I come inside you, simultaneously releasing one of my trademark farts, and you are overcome by the smell, possibly distracted by the noise, if there is any — "

"Sir, that is quite enough!"

He gets up off the couch and stomps toward the office door. "It was a mistake coming here, I never should have stopped. Don't worry, I'll leave my name and address with your secretary, should you choose to bill me, even though I've been here only a matter of minutes. I really can't see where you've assisted me in any way, and I would think you'd agree with that assessment, but nevertheless, nevertheless," and quickly he leaves, not really finishing his sentence but feeling as if he's made his point *nevertheless,* and he slams the door behind him, not wanting to hear another word from her or any other doctor.

So he lurches from his fifth bar of the day to the sixth, or maybe from the sixth to the seventh, he can't be sure at this point, but it doesn't matter, he is interested only in drowning his libido in an ocean of booze, though this is proving to be a more arduous task as he ages; his conspiratorial mind and organs are on to this trick, making it nearly impossible for him to get drunk in a truly nonfunctional sense. After all, he has been in training as a drinker since his college days, and at age

thirty-five he can polish off an entire case of beer while remaining reasonably cogent and lively.

The sun has set, and as he enters this latest watering hole he notes that the familiar night life is beginning to emerge. He takes an empty seat at the bar, catching sight of numerous women he's been with in recent months. They never say hello. They want nothing to do with him. They snicker among themselves, when in small groups, turning their backs on him, occasionally giving him disdainful looks over their shoulders. Sometimes one of them will tap a friend on the arm

— a potential sex partner for him — whisper something in her ear, and together they will regard him with revulsion, making him realize an opportunity for him is lost before it could start.

He doesn't even have time to order a drink before a woman dressed mainly in leather walks up to him from out of the smoky murkiness.

"Buy a girl a drink?" she asks, and immediately Ralph's spirits are buoyed. He has seen this good-looking brunette numerous times in taverns over the past year or so, although she always arrives alone and has never left twice with the same man.

"Why not?" he says, ordering each of them a beer. The girls who like beer are always the best — happier, more honest, unhindered by trends or annoying political concerns.

They talk. He tells her his name and learns that hers is Melissa. As they finish off several drinks, he unsuccessfully tries to remember the name of the last woman he picked up in a bar, but he cannot.

Finally she sets aside her third or fourth empty beer can — he can't recall exactly how many she's had; his ability with numbers dwindles the more he drinks — and says, "Let's go to my place."

She grabs his arm and pulls him toward the exit. She cuts a path that goes right by the woman who fled his place the night before, and he flips her off, failing to stir the slightest reaction from her. Melissa arrives at the door and pushes it open. Quickly he finds himself sitting beside the leather-clad beauty in her Porsche. He takes stock of her thighs, the

mini-skirt becoming even more provocative as it slides up the car seat and exposes the solid, milky flesh above the black pantyhose, and in what seems like no time whatsoever — or maybe he is wavering in and out of consciousness, maybe he is more drunk than he thought — he stands naked in her condo, watching her undress.

"I have this problem," he mumbles, finally wanting to come clean with a woman before actually engaging in an erotic coupling, but she makes small talk over his own comments, and ultimately he is glad she has cut him off, because she is unbelievably gorgeous, and he wants a chance at her. Better to keep his mouth shut. His customary hormones bluster more furiously than expected. Before she can remove the skimpy panties or lingerie or high heels, he wraps his arms around her and backs her down onto the bed, spreading her legs, sliding her panties to one side and entering her. They lunge against each other for several minutes and then begin to climax simultaneously.

"BRRRUUUUUUM!" his buttocks announces.

"BRRRRAAAAAAP!" explodes Melissa, and it is undoubtedly the loudest, longest belch Ralph has ever heard. Her rank breath wafts into his face, but he accepts it, he does not care, because at least she has achieved orgasm.

As she struggles to regain her breath, she touches Ralph's cheek and says, "You see, I have this problem with gas, with burping, that seems to happen when — "

"I know, I know," says Ralph, smiling at Melissa and licking perspiration from her shoulder, "I've heard that sort of thing is going around, but I'm positive we can work things out."

The organized, focused individual is, to say the least, irritated by somebody who.has no direction in life. Such an aimless person, while perhaps perfectly harmless, might come to be viewed as a threat to someone who plans and, um, executes those plans.

JAKE OSSINGER'S FULL LIFE

As fresh snow begins to fall outside the lodge, I think back to when I first met Jake Ossinger, some fifteen years ago. It was while I was playing pool at the Headquarters, a large, dusky nightclub in Elkhart, Indiana. I had just finished beating my third opponent in a row when this burly, red-bearded fellow approached the table.

"Some mighty fine shots there, my friend," he said, extending an arm.

I shook his hand, which, like the rest of his body, was massive. Large and imposing as he was, though, I noticed his face possessed a harmless childlike quality.

"Jake Ossinger," he said by way of introduction. "How about a game?"

Conversation had to be brief and screamed, thanks to the unreasonably loud heavy metal music of the latest local group, Irradiated Pond Scum or something like that, so all I said was, "Sure, but not for money."

Jake laughed heartily. "Course not."

"Rack 'em," I said, kissing Melissa as she handed me my half-finished beer.

Melissa and I weren't yet married when I met Jake, but we'd been going together for about six months. We were madly in love. We'd met in a watering hole closer to downtown. Melissa was living proof that you could indeed find a decent girl in a bar, in spite of what everybody said. Anyone can get lonely and go to a bar for a drink now and then. And while Melissa wasn't exactly lonely that night

127

at Bunko's, she was alone, and that was one of the things I initially found attractive about her. She was secure in her solitude, a characteristic I admired but rarely noticed in women who were by themselves in social settings.

She exchanged friendly small talk with some men that night I met her, and occasionally she agreed to a dance. Eventually I made my own move. The rest, as they say, is history.

"And who might this gorgeous lady be?" asked Jake, ogling Melissa as he ambled nearer to her.

Melissa normally smiled at such compliments, but I think she was overwhelmed by Jake's size. She could only stare wordlessly at his thick arms and round belly, which threatened to pop the buttons off his flannel shirt.

"Jake Ossinger," he said, holding out his hand again. Melissa reciprocated, and in a bigger-than-life gesture that seemed perfectly natural for someone his size, he bent forward, as best his waistline would permit, and delicately kissed one of her knuckles.

"Hello, Jake," she said, regaining her capacity for speech. "Melissa Olsen."

"And what might your friend's name be? He has neglected to tell me."

"Danny Vincent," I said. "Are you ready to play?"

Jake turned his attention from Melissa to the triangle of billiard balls on the green tabletop. "Fire away!" he bellowed.

So Jake and I played while Melissa watched. She didn't play pool. She never got involved in contests of any sort whatsoever, athletic or otherwise, unless they were challenges she set for herself, to be met on her own terms: running or swimming to stay in shape; reading classics of literature or listening to Mozart to improve herself culturally; throwing away a full pack of cigarettes two or three times a year and declaring again that she was kicking the habit.

By the time I was done shooting, I had knocked in three stripes. I was surprised to see Jake screwing together his own cue. It was an exquisite stick — an ivory job that had probably cost him six or seven hundred bucks, by the look of it — but what was a guy doing with it in a joint like this, where half the house sticks didn't even have tips? Everybody who played pool at the HQ was an amateur, myself included. Now it looked like Jake might turn out to be a hustler of some sort.

What followed was even more surprising than Jake's custom-made cue.

He couldn't have knocked in a ball to save his life.

On his first shot he hit the cue ball off the table. The guy I had just beaten, who stood watching nearby, grabbed the ball as it bounced across the cement floor. He lobbed it over to me.

"I met Minnesota Fats a few weeks ago," Jake was saying. "In Miami. He was playing in some tournament. We ate lunch together one day, and I told him of my interest in the game. That's why I bought this stick. To make myself a better player." Jake massaged his beautiful cue affectionately.

I dropped another stripe into a corner pocket — a tough bank shot, necessary for getting around his 2 and 3 balls — but then blew an easy straight-in attempt.

"Yes, sir," said Jake as he grunted and groaned down into position in order to shoot, "I've been playing a lot of pool since my trip to Miami. I actually believe I've found my life's calling."

He scratched in a side pocket. If pool was his "life's calling," there was room for improvement.

I was allowed to place the cue ball anywhere behind the dot, but I was damned if I could find a decent shot anywhere. I finally decided to try and sink the 9 ball.

"That Minnesota Fats is one nice guy. A marvelous sense of humor, and a gentleman too."

Jake had started talking the moment I had taken my shot. No doubt I would have failed to make the 9 even in the event of silence on Jake's part, but his loud yelling hadn't helped my efforts at concentration. Oh, well, I wasn't the one who was going to teach him about pool etiquette. If he took up the game for a living, he would learn how to behave soon enough.

"I sold practically everything I owned to pay for this baby," Jake said, tapping the cue. "All I've got left are the clothes on my back and an old clunker of a car that barely runs." Jake laughed that hearty laugh again. "Yeah, it'll be a wonder if that crazy Ford makes it through the winter. But Minnesota offered to provide me with some pointers on how to improve my game. I plan to see him again in Vegas, and I'll get there even if I have to take a damned bus. Once I develop my game, I should be able to make some good money."

"Your shot," I said, growing tired of hearing him wind off.

The next time Melissa and I ran into Jake Ossinger was two years later, in Santa Monica, California. She and I had celebrated our first wedding anniversary eight months before, and we had come a long way, in more than purely geographic terms, since meeting in the Midwest. I had leapt the journalistic fence from newspaper reporting for a low-paying, small-town ragsheet to public relations work for an average-paying, big-city university. Melissa had received a national fellowship in aerospace engineering. We had a swell apartment in Westwood. Upon relocating to southern California, it was impossible for us to immediately find a place in Santa Monica, the area we liked best, what with everybody and his brother on the waiting list for rent-controlled apartments. Nevertheless, our future looked bright.

It was Melissa who recognized Jake on the beach. He held a yellow bucket, and the ocean caressed his ankles as a dozen children danced around his broad frame.

"I know that man," said Melissa, leaning against my shoulder as we walked in Jake's direction. We had our arms wrapped around each other. "Why do I know him?"

I had gulped down a couple of beers up at Moby's Dock, and though I wasn't drunk, I was beginning to think I was a comedian. "King Kong?" I asked, pointing at Jake. "You recognize him?"

"King Kong didn't have red hair."

The man was definitely bursting with redness. The curly torch on top of his head was outdone only by the flame lapping downward from his chin and the prairie fire raging across his expansive chest.

"Where have we seen him before?" asked Melissa, poking me in the ribs.

I pulled away from her jabbing finger, and then we grabbed each other anew. "How do I know? Whadaya mean, 'we'?"

"We were together. We met this man when we were together. And it was at night."

I was preparing to argue this point good-naturedly with Melissa when King Kong yelled, "Danny! Melissa!"

He waved wildly at us. The children around him were suddenly confused. King Kong was their god, and his acknowledgment of us forced the children to accept Melissa and me as their demigods, even if they did so grudgingly.

"Jake!" exclaimed Melissa, gleefully kicking sand in the air as she finally remembered King Kong's real name. She turned to me. "His first name is Jake, and you played pool with him one night at Bunko's."

"The Headquarters," I corrected. "Bunko's didn't have a pool table."

"Right! You remember?"

I nodded slowly. "I think he's the guy who fed us that bullshit about meeting Minnesota Fats."

"Yes!"

We trotted over to Jake, the children parting to allow us access to their crimson deity.

Jake and I shook hands, and then he bent forward and kissed Melissa on the cheek, fluttering his fingers in the air as he did so.

"What are you doing here?" inquired Melissa.

"I was about to ask you the same question," said Jake, laughing heartily.

Ah, the laugh, the hearty laugh. *That* I remembered.

"We live here," said Melissa. "Dan's in public relations, and I'm a grad student."

"Beauty as well as brains," said Jake, smiling that boyish smile at Melissa.

"So what about you?" I asked Jake.

"Me? Why — " He raised the bucket up to his waist level and shook it. "Shells, my boy, shells! *Sea*shells!"

Melissa and I peeked into the bucket, which was nearly full of seashells of varying shades of brown and gray.

"Finish the story about the whale!" pleaded one of the children, a bright-eyed, fuzzy-headed African American girl.

"Soon, soon," said Jake, kneeling down among the children.

Jake explained to the children that Melissa and I were old friends of his. "So I'm going to talk to them for just a tad, and tonight we'll gather 'round the fire, the same as we did last night, and I'll finish the story of the whale. Now go collect some more shells!"

The tots erupted noisily, happily, as they scattered in every direction.

"Jake," said Melissa, obviously impressed, "you sure have a way with kids."

The three of us plopped down on the wet sand.

"Children are an easy audience for telling stories," said Jake. "Everything in the world is new to them. What's really tough is the publishing industry."

Neither Melissa nor I had a clue as to what he was talking about.

"Yeah, since we first met, I believe I've found my life's calling: I'm destined to be a writer. Can you believe it?"

We all laughed.

"I spend a lot of time on the road," Jake continued, "and reading has always been a favorite hobby of mine — in motels, in restaurants, on the interstates. I've had two or three minor car wrecks because my attention wasn't necessarily on the road, where it should have been, but that's beside the point. The thing is, the more I read, the more I thought, Hey, I could write stories too. So I invested my last dime in a cheap PC, and I began churning out chapters. I wrote an entire mystery novel in less than two months. Writing it wasn't so tough, but selling it has proven to be another story, if you'll pardon the pun."

Melissa said, "You actually wrote a book?"

"A book that won't sell!" boomed Jake, laughing some more. "But I'll keep trying."

"What about Minnesota Fats?" I asked.

"Oh, the billiards dream," said Jake, jabbing a finger into the dense sand. "I decided the game wasn't for me, no matter how good I became. How famous are even the very best pool players? Not very. So I moved on to something else."

And he had ended up in California. He had said it himself: he was always on the road. Some people never settled down. I wondered if Jake was running away from something or someone. He didn't strike me as the criminal type, but these days you never knew. What, if anything, was he searching for? He didn't seem to have any single, driving interest urging him onward, like a carrot in front of a horse.

My wife became more beautiful to me as time went on. She loved me, and I loved her, and nothing else mattered.

Most of the people we knew from the old days had gotten married and divorced, some of them two or three times. Melissa and I were solid. We fit together perfectly, like two adjoining pieces of a puzzle.

These were my happy thoughts during the period when Melissa and I encountered Jake for the third time.

We were amazed, that third time, to spot Jake at the fringe of Olympic National Park, feeding an adult black bear from the palm of his hand.

"These encounters with Jake are becoming scarily coincidental," said Melissa, sounding almost irritated as she pressed her cigarette butt into the bottom of the car's ashtray.

"Melissa, my God, he's feeding a bear, sitting there calmly, like he's not a bit scared."

She noticed I'd stopped the Mercedes and looked at me sternly. "What are you doing?"

I cupped her chin in my hand and turned her face back toward our huge acquaintance. "That's Jake out there. Our buddy Jake! We've got to say hi."

"Dear, that's also a bear out there. A *bear! Not* our buddy. You happened to mention it yourself a few moments ago."

"Yeah, but look at him. He looks pretty tame. At worst, he'll get scared and run off when we get out of the car. You watch."

"All right," she said, "but if you ask me, this business of running into Jake every few years is getting to be a little spooky — and as you know, I'm *not* superstitious."

We climbed out of the car. Upon slamming the doors shut, the bear concluded the area was becoming too crowded and, exactly as I'd predicted, ran off into the nearby trees.

Jake recognized us immediately. "Randy! Melissa! Fancy meeting you here."

Mustering every ounce of energy he had in him, Jake heaved himself to his feet and gave us each a massive hug, which finally brought a smile to Melissa's face.

"I'll bet you didn't give that bear a hug when it lumbered up to you," I said, laughing.

"Actually I did," said Jake. "The beasts don't seem to be as dangerous as a lot of folks claim. I don't know, maybe it's just me. That's the fourth bear I've fed in three days."

The older Jake got, the curlier his red hair became: his beard was fuller, his brows were bushier, and his chest — judging by the tufts of redness that pushed their way out of his shirt, in the spaces between the buttons — was more over-grown. Life seemed to be treating Jake well. He was big, as always, but he seemed comfortable with his size, a man on whom the fat didn't appear to be a burden to him.

"What brings you to Oregon?" he asked.

"Vacation," I said.

Jake gently pushed Melissa and me aside and scanned the distance back to our car. "No kids yet?" he asked.

"Nope," said Melissa. "Why do you ask?"

"I just figured you'd have little ones by now."

"My maternal instinct isn't that strong," she said. "Besides, there are already too many people in the world. Not enough jobs. So much danger and ugliness. Danny and I have a wonderful life by ourselves."

I hastened to fill in the awkward silence that ensued. "Uh, kids, yeah — all those kids on the beach. I remember that. You like children, don't you?"

"Not particularly," he said. "I don't *dis*like them, mind you, it's simply that I tend to think of myself as a big kid, so I identify with them sometimes."

"What about a woman?" asked Melissa. "Aren't you ever going to get married?"

A pained look flickered briefly across Jake's face, followed by a feeble laugh. "One of the lady forest rangers has brought me breakfast a couple of times. I don't know, maybe she's got her eye on me."

She patted Jake's cheek. "And do you have an eye for her?"

"Not really," Jake answered nervously, pulling at his beard. It was obvious he wanted to change the subject. "But I've been thinking about the possibility of becoming a forest ranger. For the past three weeks I've been wandering around this huge park, mostly living off the land, watching the sun come up, catching enough fish to feed the bears as well as myself. I think I'd like to be a forest ranger."

I didn't even have to ask Jake about the writing career he had decided to pursue the last time we saw him. He had lost interest in being a writer, just as he'd abandoned the idea of becoming a professional pool player before that. Had he ever been truly interested in anything? Probably not. I doubted he'd ever apply himself to becoming a forest ranger either.

The fourth and final time we met up with Jake was at a ski resort near Pine, Colorado, an hour or so outside of Denver. Jake was trying to ski — and having a terrible time of it.

"It's Jake," grumbled Melissa as we made our way from the car to the lodge. She pointed at a huge red blob tumbling down a nearby hill in a flurry of white powder, carving an erratic rut in the snow as a pair of skis flew up in the air like improperly fired missiles. "What's he doing here? I don't believe it."

Jake was at least a hundred yards away from us, so I couldn't imagine how Melissa had known it was him. But somehow she had been able to tell. As the flailing Jake rolled closer, I could see she was right.

"God, this is weird," I said. "Every time we take a vacation we run into him."

"Pretty soon we'll have to adopt him," Melissa said with a sneer.

After the park rendezvous of a few years earlier, Melissa and I had discussed Jake at great length. It bothered her, especially, to see a life as unguided as his, a life so totally without purpose. She did admit that Jake fascinated her "in a sad sort of way." Her own life didn't lack structure, nor did the life of the man she had married. NASA paid her a quarter of a million dollars a year for important blueprints, and I had received twice that for my last movie screenplay. She engineered, I wrote, and that was more or less the way we'd always planned it.

Jake was an unknown. What did he want out of life? What would he do next? Melissa and I didn't know, largely because Jake himself didn't know.

He was still plummeting down the hill when Melissa and I entered the lodge and checked in. She was tired from the drive and wanted to go up to the room and lie down. I said okay and found the nearest pool table. My latest movie was selling lots of tickets at the box office, and I was feeling cocky enough to kick some butt in billiards.

After winning my twelfth game in a row — I was as amazed as anyone at my streak — I retired gracefully and headed up to the room, where I figured Melissa would be sound asleep.

She was in bed, but she wasn't sleeping.

And she wasn't alone.

The drapes were drawn, and Melissa had placed a candle next to the bed. She liked having sex by candlelight. Jake, because of his size, was on the bottom, and Melissa straddled him. She flexed the muscles in her thighs and rubbed her forearms against his hairy chest, nibbling his neck as he groaned like an injured linebacker.

I couldn't make sense of what I was seeing. What did it mean? Melissa and I had a wonderful relationship. Neither of us had ever cheated on the other one, I was certain of it. Was she having sex with Jake out of pity? Did she feel sorry for him for being a lonely guy? Over the years she'd grown increasingly irritated at running into Jake so frequently, yet here she was, fucking him. Perhaps she figured, in some convoluted way, that by letting Jake briefly attach himself to her in such an intimate manner, she'd get him to flee us in the same way that he'd abandoned pool playing and writing and everything else in his unstructured life. Maybe she thought this coupling would break some peculiar spell that kept causing our paths to cross.

Melissa had left the door to our room unlocked and open a crack, as if she deliberately wanted me to see what was going on. Did she want me to do something? If so, what?

Jake had probably never made love to a woman in his life, and surely not with a stunning beauty like my Melissa.

Quietly I backed out of the room, returned the door to its original position, and stood there in the hallway, struggling to control my breathing. I wanted to rush into the room and beat the hell out of Jake with a blunt object, but I restrained myself. I knew Melissa didn't want me to do that.

I went back downstairs, entered the bar, and drank a lot. I played some more pool, winning six more games. That made me feel somewhat better.

Somewhat.

"The past several days," said Jake, his beard sprinkled with snow, "I've been thinking that maybe this is the kind of thing I could do professionally."

He meant skiing. I told myself he had to be kidding.

Jake and I stood at the top of one of the higher slopes, where I had coaxed him to accompany me. We wore our ski outfits and Nordikas. The lodge far below appeared as nothing more than a tiny brown square stitched into a huge white quilt. Off to the right were some small hills that the successful skier traversed in order to wind his way back down to the lodge. On the left were two expert downhill runs that eventually led into a wooded area that, from our vantage point, was invisible behind a shroud of morning fog.

"Jake," I said, "you're almost forty years old, and you're not exactly fit to ski professionally. So don't be ridiculous."

Jake seemed uneasy in my presence. After what he'd done with my wife yesterday afternoon, that was understandable.

"Jake, haven't you ever wanted to do anything for more than five minutes, figuratively speaking? Have you ever seriously thought about applying your life to any one thing? Like a goal?"

Almost talking over me, he said, "It's just that I've been watching you ski the past hour or two, and I think you could give me some pointers, help me master the sport. How about it?"

Jake Ossinger would never be anything, I concluded, except a dangerous unknown. An x factor. More than likely he wasn't even a good lover, though I would never know, because I would never ask Melissa.

My wife and I had vacationed at the lodge on previous occasions, and we had heard that amateur skiers, drunk or not, sometimes died in the wooded area currently enveloped by fog. They sped down the two extended runs, building up tremendous speed, and by the time they reached the timber-lined ski trails, they were racing along so fast that they lost control and killed themselves by slamming into the big pine trees.

"Don't forget to snowplow," I said, pointing the tips of my skis ever so slightly outward, which was the opposite way for snowplowing. With the ski fronts aimed away from each other, a skier would keep going, not stop. "If you find yourself going too fast, you can come to a stop by snowplowing."

Jake jabbed his poles repeatedly into the densely packed snow, anxious to get started. "All right," he said, and for a moment I thought he was going to say something else. But he didn't. Instead he slid his goggles down over his eyes and licked his lips.

"Angle over that way if you can," I said, gesturing to the left — to the fog — as I spoke.

"Got it," he mumbled.

With the encouragement of a sudden, mighty gust of wind at our backs, Jake and I pushed off and headed down the hill.

I expected him to fall within seconds and ruin my plan entirely, but to my astonishment, he stayed up on his skis, heading toward the trees.

I allowed him to get about twenty yards ahead of me. I was about twice that distance to his right, intending to ski back to the lodge as soon as I had Jake well on his way.

Thanks to his weight and the route he took, Jake was skiing faster than I had ever skied. Only yesterday I had watched him roll down the hill like a laughable incompetent. Today, though, he appeared to really have his heart in doing this one thing excellently.

"Go, Jake, go!" I yelled, turning toward the lodge. I waved my poles into the air, cheering him on into the woods.

"Hey, Danny!" he called back, sounding scared. "This snowplow business doesn't seem to be working!"

I pretended not to hear him. In fact, we were far enough apart — and the wind was blowing so noisily — that I was surprised I *had* heard him.

He waved his arms wildly as he veered into the outer fringes of the fog, traveling, I guessed, at least seventy miles an hour. It was an absolute fluke in the workings of the universe that he hadn't fallen by now.

I thought about Melissa. She would have been relieved by this turn of events, finding solace in the knowledge that I was removing the unknown tumor of Jake Ossinger from our lives. I believed she wanted it that way. She had intended for me to catch Jake and her together.

Even if I were wrong about all that, I would never know, because I would never ask.

I watched Jake disappear completely into the thick fog.

I sliced sharply to the right, twin streaks of snow flying upward behind me as I closed in on the lodge and my loving wife.

Kent Robinson

Here's another story in which, as with "Garrett Gosch Is Green," there is meant to be some comedy interwoven with tragedy.

For the record, I have nothing against parrots, and you can parrot me on that statement.

PARROT FLOP

"You're mowing in too far," yelled Clyde Simpson.

As he extracted his huge frame from the small car, he swung his briefcase wildly at Cecil Wagner, his next-door neighbor to the east. Although old lady Turner to the west wasn't a problem, Clyde had long ago embraced the philosophy that fences were the best neighbors. Clyde hated Wagner's guts. Wagner had been fooling around with his wife. He was sure of it.

Wagner started to turn the Wheel Horse in the opposite direction, seemingly oblivious to Clyde and the briefcase he brandished. The weight of the briefcase and its contents propelled Clyde over to the metal lid that covered the blades of the stubby tractor. He halted his progress just before his toes slipped under the lid, where they would have been sliced to bits. As it was, grass trimmings streamed out onto his pants and expensive wingtips.

"Hey, Wagner."

Wagner shut off the mower and reduced the engine speed while Clyde brushed himself off.

"Sorry, neighbor. What's up?"

Lately Wagner had seemed friendlier than usual. Typical of someone who doesn't want to get caught under the cloud of sexual suspicion, thought Clyde.

"You're mowing part of my lawn," Clyde informed him. "I'll mow my own lawn."

"Are you sure?" asked Wagner, getting that dumb, innocent look on his face that Clyde had seen before. His eyes grew wide, and his lips parted like the spreading fronds of a sea anemone moments before gobbling up some unsuspecting fish. Clyde wanted to poke out those eyes and stuff a rag into that gaping mouth.

"Yes, I'm sure," said Clyde. "I don't mean to be too territorial here, but please observe." He pointed to one of the clothesline posts cemented into his back yard. The other post was out of sight behind the house. "And look here," he continued, indicating a decorative rock not ten feet from the mower in the other direction. "If you draw a line between those two points, you have, roughly speaking, the line that separates our properties. You're mowing at least five feet into my lawn."

"All right. Sorry."

Clyde turned toward his house as Wagner started up the mower again.

Now he had to go inside and deal with his wife.

He kicked a tire of his cheap compact car as he stomped up the driveway. Damned piece of junk. It was less than a year old, yet no amount of servicing could make it run well. Often it stalled during rainstorms. He wished he could afford a better car — a big luxury car or even something comfortably mid-size — but Janet wasted far too much money on impulse buying to allow that. She had a wardrobe that was threatening to burst the walls of the bedroom closet. And there were all those expensive trips to the veterinarian with that stupid parrot. The damned vet was bleeding them dry. Someday Clyde would have to stop and have a few words with that mealy-mouthed bandit. The parrot was never sick. Why were all these appointments necessary? Day after day it was the same old bird, tiresomely healthy and animated, ignoring Clyde as if he didn't exist yet repeating everything Janet said, much to her infantile delight. She would squeal amusedly and offer the bird some food as a reward, saying, "Good Clarence, good Clarence!" Clarence. What the hell kind of name was that for a parrot? Or any animal, for that matter.

Why did Janet have to be allergic to dogs? Clyde believed dogs were the finest creatures on the face of the Earth. They were loyal, they were grateful for being fed, and they had true personality. Clyde had never met a dog he didn't like.

When he entered the kitchen through the garage, he heard Janet in the living room, talking to the parrot as if they were both dumb children.

"Hi, cutie! What's up?"

"'Hi, cutie! What's up?'" twittered the parrot.

Clyde let his briefcase fall from his hand. It crashed noisily onto the kitchen tiles. He hoped the bird, which Clyde could not see from where he stood, had been startled by the noise.

"I'm home, dear," he called.

Janet erupted with a squeal that could have indicated surprise or orgasm or perhaps pain, and then she scampered into view. As he stared at his pudgy, smartly dressed wife, Clyde was certain he no longer loved her, in fact doubted he ever had. Maybe she had been correct when, during one of their recent fights, she had accused him of being a misanthrope who was incapable of loving anyone. At the moment he didn't know or care.

He couldn't recall why he had married her. Surely there was a better woman for him somewhere. For the time being, though, the knot was still tied. She remained a stone around his neck, a presence in his house — would probably end up owning the blasted house if he ever mustered the energy and courage to file for a divorce.

She hugged him briefly, then kissed him on the cheek. "Hi, dear, how was your day."

The words were a statement, not a question, which told Clyde she really didn't care how his day had gone. That was fine, considering he didn't feel like getting into it.

"That idiot Wagner — "

"Oh, don't start in on Mr. Wagner again," she told him. "You just walked in the door."

Mr. Wagner, he thought bitterly. I'll bet you don't call him that when you're in the sack together.

"The son of a bitch is mowing our lawn as well as his."

Janet picked up his briefcase and placed it on the kitchen counter. "It's only grass. You don't need to swear."

Clyde grabbed a beer out of the refrigerator.

"I finally got Clarence to say 'mailman,'" said Janet. "Then I couldn't get him to stop. It was so funny!"

"Mailman! Mailman!" shrieked Clarence from the living room.

Janet laughed. Clyde loosened his tie as he strolled into the living room. The gaudy green parrot with clipped wings was out of its cage and inching its ugly prehensile feet along the frame of a generic painting of a Midwestern countryside scene that his wife had bought, on the spur of the moment, at a discount store. Clyde hated the painting almost as much as the parrot.

But at least the painting didn't imitate a ringing telephone.

Clarence was probably the only parrot alive that could deliver a realistic impression of a ringing phone. The bird's phone noise had faked them out on numerous occasions. It enraged Clyde but never failed to titillate Janet.

"Oh, isn't that cute?" she would say, giggling at Clyde, who inevitably wound up standing by his favorite recliner, next to where the phone was located, with the receiver pressed against his ear.

Clyde collapsed into the recliner. From the small table to his left, he grabbed the TV remote lying next to the phone and punched on the evening news. Then he pushed himself back in the chair as far as he could go. He glanced at the parrot.

"Janet, your bird is shitting all over the Midwest."

She came into the living room and looked at Clarence, whose dribblings streamed down across a blue sky and into a wheat field. "Oh, isn't that funny?" she said.

Yeah, thought Clyde. Hilarious. He wondered what broiled parrot tasted like, or even if parrots were edible.

The lightning must have knocked out the phones, Janet concluded as she lowered the receiver back into its cradle. It was just as well; she had heard it wasn't safe to talk on the telephone during a storm.

She thought she heard, above the rain, the scuffle of shoes on the front sidewalk. Peering out the screen door, she saw a blurry gray mass begin to take shape.

"That God-damned car," growled Clyde as he flung open the door and stomped inside, rain dripping from his hat and coat. "That's the last straw."

"What happened, dear?"

"'What happened, dear?'" repeated Clarence. The parrot was maneuvering atop the bookcase, picking at itself.

"I'm going to buy a new car first thing tomorrow," said Clyde, "whether we can afford it or not." He removed all of his clothes except his underwear, leaving them in a soppy pile on the floor. "The car died again. This time I think it died for good. I was about halfway to the office. I tried for half an hour to get it started again, but no luck. I sat there for another half hour without seeing a single cop car or tow truck. They're never around when you need them. I decided to walk home rather than die of old age sitting in that piece of shit, and naturally I didn't have my umbrella. So here I am. I swear to God, I'm going to sell that car for scrap metal."

Suddenly he had a violent coughing fit, his face turning red. "I'll probably end up with pneumonia, thanks to this whole ordeal."

"What about work?"

"'What about work?'"

"Shut that bird up," said Clyde, "or I'll take a meat cleaver to it."

"Clyde Simpson! Don't you dare even *think* such a thing!" Janet waved a hand at the parrot. "Clarence, settle down."

"'Clarence, settle down.'"

Clyde approached the parrot and reached toward it menacingly. "Polly want fast-acting poison?"

Clarence fluttered its wings and took a step back.

"Stop that," his wife told him. "You get changed, and I'll call a taxi to come take you to work."

"To hell with it. That new accountant I told you about — Withers — has been getting on my nerves lately. A day off will do me good. I'll call in sick. Withers can do the God-damned work for a change, instead of sitting around all day long talking about what should be done."

"How are you going to call in? The phone is dead. I just tried it."

"Oh?" He glared at her. "Who were you calling?" Probably that butt hole Wagner, he thought. Whether Clyde loved his wife or not, he resented Wagner thinking he could fool around with her.

"My sister," said Janet.

Clyde blinked. "What?"

"I tried to call my sister."

He nodded, then pulled a towel out of the hallway linen closet and dried himself off. "Well," he said, "if the phone's out, you can't very easily call for a taxi, can you?"

"Yes, that's true, now that you mention it."

He grabbed the heavy quilt off the couch and wrapped himself in it as he sank into his trusty recliner. Kicking back, he said, "Ah, this is perfect. The living room is dark and warm, and the sound of the summer rain already has me feeling relaxed. I didn't get much sleep last night, so a nap is just what the doctor ordered."

"But — but won't they fire you for not showing up for work?"

"Hell, no," he said. "I've got plenty of sick days built up."

"But are you really sick?"

Clyde was tired of his wife's incessant questioning. Soon he would absolutely have to get a divorce, even if he did have to surrender the house. He just couldn't take it any longer.

The immediate problem, he suspected, was that Janet was expecting a visit from Wagner. By staying home, he had ruined his wife's plans. That's why she was whining so much, urging him to make another effort to get to work.

Wagner. The worthless swine. He was always home. Didn't he have a job of some sort? Now that he thought about it, Clyde couldn't recall what Wagner did for a living. Had he ever mentioned it? Maybe he was independently wealthy, which would be one explanation for Janet's interest in him, being the big spender she was.

He said, "Dear, I predict that, due to my unhealthful exposure to the elements mere minutes ago, I will be extremely physically ill by midafternoon. And even if I'm not, who cares? Nobody at the office will know the difference. Nor would they care if they did know; everybody calls in sick now and then, even if they're not. It's an American tradition."

Janet stared sternly down at him, her arms folded across her breasts. "You're becoming seriously withdrawn," she said. "You didn't used to be this way."

"That's ridiculous," he said. "I just want to rest and have a day off. Now leave me alone. And keep that stupid bird quiet."

Janet wandered off into another part of the house, and Clyde drifted into sleep. As he went deeper and deeper, he sensed it would be a long, refreshing sleep, the kind he had experienced often as a worry-free child. He hoped his cough didn't rattle him awake, because he wanted to escape the day for as long as possible. Flee all thoughts of work and Janet and his pathetic marriage to her.

He'd frequently thought that the marriage had run out of steam years ago and these days merely coasted downhill, proceeding inexorably to its lowest point. They never went anywhere or had friends over. They never made love, and when she bothered to kiss him on the cheek, it was like being licked by some sort of reptile. Nothing was original or exciting anymore.

He wasn't sure if he had fallen asleep, but he felt as if his conscious self had flowed out of his mind and was hovering above him. He could see himself lounging in the recliner. He was awake in the chair, talking to himself. He told himself he would file for divorce by the end of the week. He couldn't handle being responsible for another human being. He wasn't made for marriage. Neither, apparently, was Janet, since she had been unfaithful. At least he wasn't guilty of that, though God knows he had been tempted more and more lately.

Clyde wanted to sleep forever, to hibernate for eternity in this dream in which he was finally making some firm, rational decisions about his future.

But the phone was ringing. He couldn't tell how long it had been ringing, but it was loud — loud and insistent, like an alarm. Where was Janet? Why didn't she answer it?

Even before he was fully awake, Clyde extended his hand toward the table next to the recliner. Vaguely, however, he seemed to remember that when the recliner was all the way back, the phone was just out of reach.

But it kept *ringing* and *ringing* and —

Utterly against his will, he shook himself awake and sat up sharply in the chair. The back of the recliner snapped forward, and Clarence, who had been perched on top of the chair, went soaring past Clyde's face as nothing more than a green streak.

In that same instant, Clyde blinked and saw a shadowy figure standing almost directly ahead, in the front doorway.

"Damn it!" barked Clyde, answering the phone and hearing only silence. Of course. The storm had cut off the power, Janet had said. Clarence had been doing his idiotic phone imitation.

The figure in the doorway yelled in agony and stumbled backward as the green streak flopped against his face. Clyde heard Clarence's confused squawk as Wagner slapped at his face and toppled out onto the front porch, knocking the screen door off its hinges as he fell backward through it.

"My eye!"

"Wagner?"

Janet entered the living room and hurried out to the porch, where the feathered remains of Clarence oozed out from beneath Wagner's right buttock.

"Clarence!" she cried, kneeling.

"Oh, God, my eye! Your parrot put out my eye!"

"So, Wagner, it's true," said Clyde, throwing aside the quilt and heaving himself out of the chair. He walked out onto the porch, hovering over Janet and the sobbing Wagner. "You've been screwing my wife, just as I thought."

"Clyde!" shrieked Janet. "For God's sake, shut up!"

"You thought I was at work, so you came over for a little action."

"I came to get some sugar."

Clyde laughed. "Right!"

"Clyde, stop it!" Janet demanded.

"That bird put my eye out," bawled Wagner.

"Don't act innocent with me, Janet," said Clyde. "I know what's been going on between you and the neighbor here."

"Look at poor Clarence," sobbed Janet.

"I'd say Clarence is history," observed Clyde. "And so is this marriage."

Janet stood and faced him.

"I've had it up to here," he told her. "I've known about you two for some time."

"Nothing's going on, Clyde."

"Don't try to pull the wool over my eyes." Clyde chuckled, nudged Wagner with his foot, and said, "Maybe I shouldn't have mentioned *eyes.* "

"That's cruel," said Janet. *"You're* cruel."

"Hey, I was just taking a nap. Minding my own business."

"Jesus Christ, would someone please help me?" pleaded Wagner.

In spite of his feelings toward the man, Clyde helped Janet lead the bloodied Wagner inside, where they seated him on the couch. After studying the wound, Clyde told Wagner he'd probably lost the eye. The late Clarence's beak had been as hard as flint.

"None of this would have happened if we had got rid of that parrot a long time ago, like I suggested," Clyde told his wife.

Janet checked the phone and discovered the power had been restored. She called for an ambulance and then rode with Wagner to the hospital.

Clyde stood in the open doorway of his house, still wearing only his underwear. He didn't care if the neighbors saw him or not. And he didn't care if Janet wanted to be with Wagner either. He just didn't care anymore, and not caring brought a feeling of liberation to him, almost as if the divorce was already over and done with.

The storm had passed, and the gray clouds were breaking up, allowing scattered rays of sunlight to filter through.

Kent Robinson

A bunch of screwballs in Chicago actually held a protest like the one in the story that follows. When I read about it in the paper, I couldn't believe it. Some people have too much time on their hands. They need to take up hobbies.

I'm glad I live in a country where protests are allowed to occur and protesters can live as freely as anyone else. But most protests I've ever read about or seen on TV irritate the hell out of me. I suppose the typical protester would tell me, "That's what they're supposed to do." Okay, then, thank you. Anyway, I think I've finally figured out why protests annoy me: they're usually a stance against something. This group is against toy weapons, that group wants to ban fur coats, those yahoos over there won't tolerate sexually explicit movies, blah blah blah.... Every time one of these groups gets its way with the passing of another restrictive law, we lose a freedom or two, and the nation is weakened.

Whatever happened to live and let live? Someone else's style of freedom doesn't have to mirror yours or meet with your approval, as long as you and your property are not being harmed or your freedoms aren't being infringed upon. Mind your own business, you fucking busybody!

Now you might say, "Of course protesters are always against things — that's why they're called protesters." But the dictionary offers at least two definitions of the word "protest," only the first — and, yes, as such, most commonly used — of which is to express a dislike or disapproval of something. The second most common definition, though, has to do with affirming something, as with, say, a protester who gets arrested and later affirms his innocence.

TOYS R FUN

He was their manager and, today, their general. With his hands clasped behind his back, Keith Rondini surveyed his clerks, his troops. His stare was steely, his posture perfect. The mother of all battles would soon begin.

Who was he kidding? He felt like a fool.

"Is everyone here?" he asked, failing in his effort to sound solemn.

"Tonya isn't," chirped Meera.

"Then Tonya no longer has a job."

His battalion of teenagers abruptly quit murmuring among themselves. *That* had gotten their attention. Whispers of warmth from the store's heating vents and the distant purl of water in Fairfield Mall's centrally located fountain were, for a weighty moment, the only detectable noises.

"When I said I needed all of you on duty today, that's exactly what I meant. Those of you not normally scheduled to be here at this time...thank you for coming."

Present, besides Meera, were Gary, Robyn, Beth, Marco, and Herbie, whom Gary liked to call "Herpes" on the rare, combative occasions when they found themselves working the same shift. Herbie's mouth always did seem to be decorated with a blister or two, but Keith was fairly certain the kid didn't have herpes or any other viral disease. What the Toys R Fun manager *did* find disconcerting about his youngest employee was that *Herbie* was his true name, written that way on his birth certificate, apparently. Not *Herbert* or even *Herb*. What the hell was the matter with parents that they would name a child *Herbie?* Didn't they realize that, as a grown-up, he would be uncomfortable with such a moniker? At age 15, the boy was already somewhat

self-conscious about his Herbie-ness.

As far as the shortcomings of parents were concerned, Keith suspected he would encounter many of them before this day was over.

"Boys and girls," he said, "we are about to go to war."

That remark, ridiculous as it was, appeared to impress Gary and Marco, who were at that stage in life where proving their manhood was a significant undertaking. Two-hundred-pound Beth looked bored. Robyn, the foxy senior with hair like shimmering corn silk, continued to smile innocently. Meera, the smart brunette, gazed condemningly at Herbie as he reached inside his pants to adjust his underwear.

"Most of you were probably too busy watching MTV last night to listen to the news — "

"VH1," interrupted Gary. "Less rap shit."

"Fine," said Keith. "Whatever. My point is, I was surprised to hear on the local news that an activist group called WANT — Weapons Are Not Toys — will be picketing our store today at noon. Should be about thirty of 'em."

"All right!" blurted Gary, and he and Marco high-fived each other.

"Perhaps they have a point," said Meera.

Keith shook his head, confused. "Perhaps *who* has a point?"

"The WANT activists. I mean, weapons *aren't* toys."

"Well...the weapons we sell *are* toys, Meera. They're *toy weapons!*"

This elemental circumlocution silenced her. She was either baffled or insulted, Keith wasn't sure which.

"Hey, Herpes, we get to duke it out with some protesters!"

Herbie removed his hand from inside his pants and stood as still and quiet as a stone.

"Gary," said Keith, "we aren't going to 'duke it out' with anybody. I merely wanted all of you here to help maintain order. Keep an eye out for shoplifters, destruction of property, that sort of thing."

"Will there be cameras?" asked Robyn, her teeth glittering, her supple limbs suddenly aquiver over the prospect of stardom.

"Media," said Keith. "Yeah, probably so. Don't get excited, Robyn; it's unlikely *Cosmo* will send a photographer."

Marco laughed.

Keith had given no consideration to the possibility of reporters showing up, but some would inevitably drop by: they circled around these activist groups like buzzards, converting silliness into so-called news. What if he received requests for interviews? He was, after all, in charge of this particular Toys R Fun outlet. Would he really have to speak in defense of the chain? He was a 32-year-old college dropout who, as a struggling sculptor, couldn't have cared less, in his heart of hearts, about Toys R Fun. He was stuck here for the worst, commonest reason: he possessed no marketable skills yet had to work *somewhere* to pay the bills. He'd slaved away at this Chicago store for three years and still couldn't get past the embarrassment. His ego was permanently bruised. How could he plug consequence and motivation into the sockets of his life? The apathy circuits just kept firing, day after agonizing day. The widespread belief that most jobs — jobs like his — were rewarding *if they were approached with the right attitude* was one of society's more torturous myths. Any idiot could manage a toy store or stand behind a cash register. It was even easier than running a fast-food restaurant, something he had done for a while in the '90s. He often wondered how people, wasting away at their meaningless occupations, kept going. In one sense he knew: people kept going by climbing out of bed each morning and wondering how people kept going. *People* meant the *rest* of humanity. The key was to absorb and relish the anguish of others while ignoring one's own or, at the very least, regarding it as minimal by comparison.

"So how do we handle these activists?" asked Gary.

Keith walked behind the counter and raised a pasteboard sign. "I came in early this morning and made this."

In red block letters the sign said:

TOY WEAPONS TEST SITE!

TODAY ONLY!

He glanced at his watch. "It's almost ten o'clock. As soon as we open the store, I'll hang this baby up front."

Keith had a plan in mind. Though inspired, it struck him as vaguely irresponsible, but he didn't care. If the activists were going to force him to defend the sale of plastic armaments — a branch of capitalism he had no opinion on, one way or the other — then he was determined to wring at least some enjoyment from the experience. Let the Toys R Fun regional director fire him; he'd simply get another dead-end job somewhere else. There were a thousand malls in the city and five thousand burger joints, and almost all of them were perpetually hiring.

"I'm also bringing in three clowns," said Keith.

"'Clowns'?" asked Meera.

Keith's teenage crew began to think the boss had gone insane, and when Floppy, Bow-wow, and Zero entered the store, they were even more convinced.

The clowns arrived at eleven. Saturday-morning cartoons still held most Chicago children in their animated spell, no doubt, but already half a dozen tots, with moms and dads in tow, were roaming up and down the aisles of Toys R Fun, examining the board games, scrutinizing dolls, inspecting whiffle bats and chemistry sets and stuffed dinosaurs.

"Remember, kids," Keith announced over the store's loudspeaker, "today you are at a weapons test site. Be sure to warn your parents. Get a gun up front, and join in on the action."

Keith had stationed Robyn and Herbie at the register. Despite her distracting beauty, she was by no means stuck-up; she didn't ignore the festering boy or address him rudely, like the others did. When they worked together, Herbie relaxed and completely abandoned the nervous habit of maneuvering his underwear. He and Robyn stood near a neatly stacked pile of blasters, grenade ejectors, bazookas, and other materiel that had been unpacked and loaded during the first hour. Beneath the jutting base of a wall ran a garden hose from the employee bathroom at the rear of the store up to a huge, green tub next to the counter, where squirt guns could be filled.

Gary and Marco had gone out into the mall to round up more kids. Meera and Beth stocked shelves and assisted customers when necessary.

"We're <u>here</u>, boys and girls!" yelled Zero the moment he and his fellow clowns entered the store in a flourish.

What good were kids with toy guns, Keith had reasoned, unless they had moving targets to stalk and fire upon?

"Zero," said Floppy, feigning annoyance, "do me a favor and shut up."

Bow-wow, down on all fours, barked loudly, like an excited dog.

Floppy's bright green shoes were two feet long. Bow-wow, who never spoke in any human tongue while clowning around, sported drooping dog ears and a shiny black nose with whiskers. Zero's expansive costume, which made him wider than the other two combined, gave him the shape of the arithmetic symbol for which he was named. The trio was an explosion of colorful clothing, wild wigs, and outlandish makeup.

Keith came out from the back room just in time to hear an unseen girl yell, "Look, Mommy! *Clowns!*"

Zero, confronting Floppy, said, "You smell like you could use a shower," and he squeezed the yellow flower on his lapel, squirting water into the other clown's face. Bow-wow let loose with another round of boisterous yelping.

"All right, wiseguy!" screamed Floppy, noticing the stack of toy weapons. While Zero swatted at Bow-wow and tried to keep the canine from biting his heels,

Floppy filled up a Super Saturator cartridge, snapped it into place on the gun, and fired at Zero, scoring a direct hit. "This is my kind of toy!" he proclaimed.

Two boys broke free from their parents and headed for the cache of weapons, where one of them grabbed a foam missile assault rifle and the other scooped up a dart gun. They started firing at the clowns and at each other.

"You'll get yours!" screeched Zero, toppling a barrel of teddy bears as he waddled down an aisle in pursuit of one of the boys.

"Come back here, Zero!" called Floppy, his striped balloon pants fluttering. "I'm not finished with you."

The boy with the dart gun chased after Bow-wow.

"Arf, arf!"

Gary and Marco returned with eight more kids, a gaggle of adults trailing behind. The youngsters immediately saw the weapons and hurried over to them.

Keith went to the back to make another announcement on the PA system: "That's right, shoppers, Toys R Fun has been declared a weapons test site! Nobody is safe! *Everybody* is fair game! Shop at your own risk!"

Herbie got whacked in the butt with a shizoku sword. Robyn squealed as pellets from a pistol ricocheted off her neck and arms.

Then, as Keith strolled toward the front of the store, he looked out into the mall and saw *them* approaching.

The activists. The monomaniacs. The card-carrying members of WANT.

Keith read their bobbing signs: WEAPONS ARE NOT TOYS, with the first letter of each word underlined and rendered in a different color than the rest of the word; THERE'S NOTHING FUN ABOUT A GUN; SAVE OUR CHILDREN — BOYCOTT TOYS R FUN; KILLING IS A TRAGEDY, NOT A GAME. The most irrational sign said, TOY GUN SELLERS SHOULD BE SHOT.

Keith met them at the broad entrance to the store. "Welcome to Toys R Fun," he said, scanning the activists. Definitely a humorless bunch, he thought. Full of righteous indignation and misguided purpose. Very likely mothers and fathers themselves. In fact, some had very unhappy-looking children accompanying them. Television and radio news teams orbited the group.

"I'm Keith Rondini," he continued, "the manager, and I must caution you that Toys R Fun has been designated a weapons test site." He reached out and patted his homemade sign.

"This is an outrage!" cried one of the activists.

"The children!" wailed another. "Oh, the poor children!"

An airy projectile from a Slayer Slingshot struck Keith in the back of his head. Girlish giggles followed. Bow-wow howled and growled incessantly. More than a dozen children raced in every direction, throwing cap grenades, waving pistols, and launching power arrows at perceived enemies. Meera dodged liquid bursts of ammunition from a pump-and-shoot hydrophaser; big Beth was not so lucky. Gary and Marco had donned sunglasses and ill-fitting, olive-colored army helmets. Floppy and Zero ran into each other and fell down. Laughter and screeches of delight erupted everywhere, mixed with exclamations of "Gotcha!" and "Aw, I'm dead!" Amid the carnage, Herbie rang up a purchase while Robyn sacked the merchandise.

"You're free to enter the store," Keith told the activists," but you do so at your own peril. You might get wet. You very well could take a rubber Nina knife in the gut; such a wound is almost always fatal. In any event, I advise you not to deliberately block the aisles, as yesterday's news reports indicated you plan to do. If you interfere with the right of the children to freely shop, I'm prepared to make citizen's arrests, for Toys R Fun does indeed carry — "

He pulled a set of plastic handcuffs out of his pocket.

" — *official police play equipment!*"

A radio reporter elbowed her way forward, identified herself, and said the comments she was getting were being taped for broadcast later on.

"How do you feel about selling toy guns to children?" she inquired.

"I have no opinion on it," Keith said.

"But you're the manager."

"Yes, I am." He hated it when reporters *insinuated* — when they substituted statements for questions.

"But don't you feel a certain responsibility to the community?"

"I guess. Since when is selling toy guns defined as irresponsible? Just because these activists say so and you, the supposedly objective reporter, adopt their position? Look, lady, I manage this lousy store for the simple reason that I can't make a living as a sculptor. I toil in unsatisfying fashion to pay the rent, the same as most of your listeners."

"That's not why I do my job, Mr. Rondini," said the reporter.

"Good for you, you mover and shaker, you. Did you want to ask me something else?"

Suddenly — unjustifiably, in Keith's view — the journalist looked offended. WANT sheep flocked into the store on either side of them as they stood there silently facing each other. Two-thirds of the WANT adults were women.

Keith stopped one lady who had her hands full with a baby rather than a sign. A lit cigarette dangled from between her lips.

"No smoking in the store," he said. It wasn't a rule he cared about or even believed in, but it was fun giving the WANT crazy a hard time.

Disgusted, she spat the cigarette onto the tile floor in front of his feet and stubbed it out. "All you're doing is promoting violence," she said.

"How so? Madam, toy stores promote play — for the purpose of profit, of course. They promote pretend. I'm no child psychologist, but I'd say pretending is an important part of growing up. Wouldn't you? It was when I was little, at least. Better that I should promote cancer?"

She didn't react to this, Keith surmised, because she probably failed to understand it. The zombie-like brain of the fanatic had no method for processing sarcasm — or, for that matter, original thinking of any sort. To zombies, there were only the catch phrases, the red-flag words, and, most importantly, the One Big Idea programmed into their heads. They found themselves thrown together as a result of a particular shared torment that was usually nothing more than a reflection of some personality defect. In the case of WANT, the One Big Idea was that society was too violent, partly because toy weapons were sold to children. Precisely because it was Big, the Idea permeated everything, filled every waking hour, polluted every cogent thought: kids failed in school because society was too violent, marriages crumbled because society was too violent, oil spills occurred in the Atlantic because society was too violent.... Violence was everywhere! It was a crisis of epidemic proportions! A *tragedy!* The news media loved that word. Eradicate violence, and you'd solve all the world's problems — except, Keith knew, the problem of the busybodies who truly *did* seem to be everywhere.

A skinny man trembling with the barely contained fury of his own anger closed in on Keith from behind. "I just think this is a God-damned shame!" he snarled without elaborating.

"Well put," Keith muttered. The man and the female reporter lingered in his vicinity. She had planted herself in front of him and had swung her microphone left and right, capturing as much of his verbal exchange with the skinny man as she'd been able to. Keith spotted a TV camera trained on him from a short distance away. He felt surrounded.

He turned and regarded the scene inside the store. Harmless chaos reigned: the hair and clothes of activists became soaked by roving children wielding deadly

Super Saturators; Zero tumbled into a corner, pinning a set of amazed parents against converging walls; Gary dangled from an overhead light; Meera and Beth slapped at Bow-wow as he nipped at their heels; Herbie, brandishing a power bow, awkwardly defended a cowering, laughing Robyn.

Again Keith reminded himself that he didn't care about Toys R Fun. And the activists and media personnel were beneath contempt, nothing but busybodies. As for the kids? If, to engage in a game of cops and robbers, children had to use their hands for guns, as in the past, then they would just point their fingers and do so without complaint, Keith knew. They passed the time in a happy world well beyond the depraved confines of politics gone awry and a sad, dangerous proliferation of Big Ideas — surely a vexing fact of life for professional whiners and their messengers on the information superhighway who fought to drag everyone down to their miserable level by distributing illusory pain equally among everyone.

Tomorrow, he knew, editorials about this incident would surface in the newspapers. Editorials about the do-gooder WANT organization and its One Big Idea. Editorials about his decision to turn the store into a toy weapons test site. Would any of the editorials see the humor of it all? Would they mention what fun the kids had playing?

Kent Robinson

Although this story is about a man consumed by a fear of terrorism, I wrote it years ago, in the 1980s, long before 9/11. Even back then I recognized terrorism as an all-too-present evil in the world, capable of ruining lives by the very fear it instills in law-abiding people.

NO ONE HAS YET CLAIMED RE- SPONSIBILITY FOR THE BOMBING

The morning news is playing when Wagner hears an assortment of sounds from upstairs. A short time later, pushing from his mind the latest violence in Sidon, he moves toward the door of his apartment as unseen rubberized wheels clatter and bounce along the floor outside his door, a few feet beyond the drab living space he occupies. Important events seem to be taking place nearly simultaneously on two adjoining levels of the complex, an observation that both frightens and intrigues him. Not since the previous shooting has there been this much excitement in the building.

It's happened again, he thinks as he flings wide his apartment door and sees the paramedics rushing across the landing with a stretcher. The guerillas have invaded, leaving a trail of blood in their wake, and the rest of us, feeling fortunate as neighbors not directly victimized, are expected to turn our backs and accept this.

"Well I absolutely refuse to accept it," proclaims Wagner with raised and shaking fist, wandering out onto the littered landing, kicking with futility at Burger King cups and candy wrappers long ago discarded. The paramedics ignore him as they climb the stairs. "Just who do they think they are, these terrorists, storming in here like unreasoning savages, killing the innocent in the name of political or religious fulfillment?"

A flurry of whiteness blossoms outside Mrs. Freeling's apartment on the floor above Wagner's, where the paramedics have halted and are unfolding a sheet. Wagner notices Kolakowski has ventured out of his unit, located next to Mrs. Freeling's and directly above his own. The ruddy-faced Kolakowski points a finger at Wagner and barks down at him a long string of obscenities, warnings against being too loud and overreacting to the situation at hand and attempting to incite some kind of riot.

Wagner has been involved in this type of exchange with Kolakowski on many previous occasions, and usually the overemotional Polish immigrant will continue to exaggerate his point. Today, however, Kolakowski's attention, like Wagner's, is drawn to the sight of Mrs. Freeling being loaded onto the stretcher like a shrunken gunnysack of dried straw.

The beloved, aged Mrs. Freeling, thinks Wagner, an inspiration to us all, a threat to no one. A humble, strong woman. Now a target of the African National Congress or some such terrorist group. How can this be? Where is the justice?

But even as Wagner ponders possible answers, Mrs. Freeling's personal nurse staggers out into the hallway, her arms swinging in every direction as if groping for the mercy of balance itself. She briefly waves in the immediate vicinity of Mrs. Freeling and then screams, "The cancer! The cancer!" Wagner can only assume the nurse has misread occurrences of the last several minutes, apparently not noticing the men with guns who undoubtedly bashed their way into Mrs. Freeling's apartment and shot her. Yet he decides it is useless to try to set straight the nurse's thinking at this point. After all, usually he barely has enough patience to deal with Kolakowski on a rational plane, and this morning, after having stocked shelves for hours, he has no patience for anyone.

The cancer, thinks Wagner bitterly as he stumbles back into his apartment. The cancer is humanity itself, although then again, then again, surely there must be some good in people. Mrs. Freeling is good. Was good. Before they blasted her life away.

Wagner does not recall changing channels on his television before stepping out of his apartment to investigate events, but this is indeed what he must have done, for now another local news program is beaming to him its phosphorescent images of terrorism from around the globe. Brutality without pattern, murder without design. It is almost more than Wagner can take, but always before he has managed to deal with his fear of becoming a victim, and he knows he will continue to do so. What other choice does he have?

"No one has yet claimed responsibility for the bombing," the silver-haired TV anchor is saying in connection with an explosion inside a crowded Istanbul syna-gogue. He delivers the line in a tone of tired resignation, as if this latest carnage is too much for him, as if he will offer forgiveness to the first fundamentalist splinter group to come forward and take credit for the bombing, so long as its members promise to never again commit such an atrocity.

"Eighteen persons are confirmed dead," reports the female co-anchor, "in a shootout between extremist factions in Muslim West Beirut." There is some confusion in switching cameras from one anchor to another, and for a moment the woman stares unwittingly off into space, as if speaking to a studio audience. But her true audience is three million viewers throughout the city, and with such an as-tronomical number of people hanging on her every word, she doesn't allow some minor directional difficulty to dampen her enthusiasm for an instant; she describes the terrorists' clash in energetic, pathetic detail, as if she has been personally, pas-sionately involved with the story and must now numb the rest of the world with grim news of the tiny war. Then both anchors turn to each other and, by way of irritating small talk, come to a brisk consensus about what a tragedy the shootout was.

"Turn down that TV!" yells Kolakowski from upstairs as the station cuts away to a commercial for G. I. Joe. The commercials are always louder than the programs, designed to grab the attention of the eager consumer.

Consumerism, thinks Wagner. That is all terrorism is, really: the ultimate in consumption. We consume so much that we eventually consume ourselves. Consumerism is definitely the word of the day.

"I'm warning you, Wagner," continues Kolakowski, apparently having re-entered his own apartment, his voice descending through Wagner's ceiling with absurd ease, "if I have to come down there and tell you again, there could be consequences."

It is not that the TV is too loud, thinks Wagner. It is that the walls and ceilings and floors of the structure are too thin. But what is to be done? Wagner, a mere night clerk at a small corner market, cannot afford to relocate, and the landlord is nothing but a shiftless rent collector who refuses to spend a dime on improvement or upkeep.

Wagner turns off the TV. He is tired of watching it anyway. Having succumbed to Kolakowski's demands, Wagner decides he'd better not hear any more complaints from him the rest of the morning. Why is Kolakowski always around? "Don't you ever work?" Wagner mumbles softly, not wanting the Pole to hear him.

He harbors some fear of Kolakowski. In a subterranean cavern of his brain, Wagner suspects that Kolakowski may very well be an inside operative for one of the countless terrorist groups. Employed by the Popular Struggle Front, perhaps. Or the Islamic Jihad. That last organization would fit Kolakowski perfectly, thinks Wagner. The surly Polack waging his own holy war in an effort to take control of the building. Mrs. Freeling was obviously a casualty of some vicious, ruthless band of terrorists; it was probably Kolakowski who engineered the killing. Kolakowski of the Islamic Jihad, finishing off the tenants, one by one.

Well you're not going to get me, you bastard, thinks Wagner as he sits down on the couch. He reaches out and opens the drawer of the coffee table in front of him. The revolver is there. While it is not exactly an arsenal and certainly no match for bombs or grenades or even submachine guns, it is nevertheless more than enough to keep Kolakowski at bay. Kolakowski, Wagner knows, is not precisely sure about his possessing the revolver, but on the other hand he's not a completely stupid creature either, and he no doubt has his suspicions. He is wary in the manner of a thuggish bulldog, but still he is wary.

Wagner lifts the newspaper off the floor and stares at a headline below the fold: "Mourners Pray for Massacred Jews." Leafing through the pages of the front section, he discovers all sorts of accounts of terrorism or, as in the case of the mourners, its aftermath. Wagner nearly expects the columns of print to turn red as he scans them.

Flinging the paper aside, he rises and strolls into the kitchen, searching for his cigarettes. He explores the cluttered counter and then feels a remote twinge of panic when he finds out he has smoked them all. Christ, he thinks, my nerves will be shot by noon.

He swears at himself for working all night long in a place that sells cigarettes and then forgetting to buy some and bring them home. He considers making a quick trip back down to the all-night market — he'll never be able to get to sleep without taking a few relaxing puffs — but questions the wisdom of such an excursion. The terrorists who killed Mrs. Freeling are probably still roaming throughout the neighborhood, searching for targets, prowling for innocent pedestrians. Why offer myself to them? he asks himself. Let them shoot some unsuspecting person out for a stroll or fire at passing cars in an attempt to crucify oblivious motorists. Wagner recalls that less than a week ago two vehicles collided in the intersection right outside the building. The authorities said it was an accident involving a drunk driver, but Wagner knows better, he knows better. He is convinced it was a meticulously timed set of circumstances — one terrorist from one group trying to annihilate another terrorist from another organization — though he was never able to sort out any clear idea as to motive or identities of involved parties.

Unable to decide whether to go to the market, he turns on the radio, which is tuned to his favorite all-news station. He will wait on an update on the situation in the area, and if it turns out that the coast is clear, he will indeed venture out to get his cigarettes.

" — yet claimed responsibility for the bombing," says the radio announcer, and despairingly Wagner wonders what terrorist account is now in progress. How many dead bodies this time? My God, he thinks, reeling to the other side of the room, terrorism surrounds us like the atmosphere, this fierce obsession with human slaughter. They wipe out my best neighbors, they incorporate the worst into their ranks, they strike down helpless citizens in the streets and the schools and the churches —

"Wagner, what's all the racket about? God damn it, how is a person supposed to have any peace and quiet with you playing the TV so loud? I warned you once. I've had enough of this, by God."

Wagner turns his face up in the direction of the ceiling. "It's the radio, you stupid Polack. And what makes you think you're king around here?" But it is too late. Wagner hears Kolakowski stomp across the living room of his apartment, heading for his door, having suddenly erupted into motion like an enraged giant. His thudding, determined steps betray his bloodthirsty purpose: Wagner knows the terrorist Kolakowski is bent on destroying him, on snuffing out his life in a much more hands-on way than he employed with Mrs. Freeling.

"We'll just see about that," mumbles Wagner, hurrying over to the coffee table, with its drawer still open, and extracting the revolver. Going to the door of his apartment, he yanks it open and leaps out onto the landing, and there is Kolakowski, descending the steps. His severe face, crippled by some undefined mental anguish, is about to register a new pain, yes, thinks Wagner, laughing. You son of a bitch, I've had it up to here with you. And as Kolakowski looks up and sees, with surprise, that his challenge is being met, Wagner raises the revolver and fires, carving a messy slice out of his midsection, sending him tumbling over the railing to his death three stories below. Wagner goes over to the railing and peers downward, gazing at the lifeless form of Kolakowski, shrunken and crumpled. "You won't hear my radio down there!" screams Wagner. "Or my TV. Or anything." Laughing some more, he returns to his apartment, where he sags against a wall, wiping sweat from his brow as earlier drops burn his eyes.

Sirens draw closer. Someone has called the police. Odd, thinks Wagner, how people are so willing to get involved from a distance, from an anonymous perspective. But the cops will enter the building and, after exhaustive and fruitless questioning, find that no one has heard, let alone seen, a thing. No bullet pierced skin, Wagner can hear himself saying, no body fell, surely not. What are you talking about, officer?

I know, thinks Wagner, I know exactly what happened, but I'm not talking, I'm not about to reveal too much, no sir, not on your life. It is the terrorists, officer, it must be them. If something has indeed happened here, the terrorists are ultimately responsible. They are everywhere. But do you think I'm going to tell you that? I don't want them coming after me. Hey, as far as I know, nothing out of the ordinary is going on around here.

As a resident of the Los Angeles area during much of the 1980s and the early 1990s, I was struck by how diligently some so-called animal rights activists worked for their cause while seeming not to notice the pitiable homeless people living (if you can call it that) among them.

Awful though it may sound, as I've gotten older I've come to realize that animals do sometimes seem more worthy of compassion than my fellow human beings. There's nothing like a good dog for companionship, loyalty, and amusement. I used to think that animals do not have feelings, but now I am pretty sure they do.

However, unless I'm mistaken, animals do not have rights. But people are prevented, by law, from doing certain things to animals.

WHALEWATCH

The cough shook him awake for the third morning in a row. Southern California nights were not yet unbearable, but he could feel the pre-dawn chill in the air that signaled impending winter; the steady drop in temperature had begun, like it did each fall, without meteorological fanfare, simply one more persistent reality with which to deal.

How many falls had it been since <u>the</u> fall? How many years? Three? Four? Ten? He had lost precise track of time long ago. It might as well have been an eternity, for all it mattered.

Sitting up on the dirt slope, he twisted his torso to the right, away from his wife, and coughed some more, trying to be as quiet as possible. But then he looked over his shoulder and saw that she was already awake, watching him.

"You okay?" she asked. She reached out a hand to his. She patted it, stroked his fingers gently. "That's a terrible cough."

"It'll pass."

He leaned down toward her, and she rolled in his direction, her legs wrapped in crummy blankets. They kissed.

He wondered what she was thinking about this morning. In some ways, she was as mysterious to him now as the day they had first met. He found that titillating, in spite of their problems. He loved her as much as ever. He was glad he had married her, in another life, so long ago.

She blinked at him and fixed his gaze with hers. He thought she could have been awake for hours, her eyes shone with such diamond vigor. She was always strong at this time of day, but within hours that strength would depart, like rain sucked into the soil. She would withdraw, her energy tapped, her eyes becoming gray and distant — a new dimension of mystery she had never exhibited until after they had lost their home.

"How was the freeway for you?" he asked. "I woke up once, when a truck went by. It was carrying a bunch of loose oil drums or something; they bounced and clanged. God, for a minute I thought we were in a war zone."

"I didn't hear anything," she said. "I slept straight through. I feel good!" She grinned and stretched her arms high above her head.

The position of the Sun gradually changed, and he saw his wife's face transformed from shadow to radiance as the light found its way over a billboard and streamed in under the overpass. he could feel the warmth soaking into his back as he stared at her illuminated features.

She slapped his shoulder playfully. "What are we going to do today?"

"Beg for food. Beg for money. Beg for attention."

She laughed, ignoring his mood.

"Aren't you freezing?" His goose bumps remained, despite the Sun's arrival.

"'Freezing'?" She buried her head in his crotch and shook it rapidly, which caused him to laugh too, though somewhat against his will. He scooted away, holding his covered genitals. "It's going to get a lot colder than this," she continued, "before it gets warmer. It's only October, as I recall."

He stood up, brushing the dirt from his pants and then his hands. he felt hungry, as usual. The hunger was always present, gnawing at his insides like insatiable termites gobbling up the walls of a house. Eventually the besieged walls would collapse under the roof's weight. How long before he and his wife met a similar fate? Surely starvation would one day claim them, and they would wake up so weak, so exhausted, that they would be unable to get off the ground and carry on with their miserable lives.

She rose beside him, the blankets falling at her feet. "Let's go watch the whales," she said.

"What for?" he asked, irritated by the idea.

"You got other plans?"

Of course he didn't, and she knew it. How could there be any plans when there wasn't any future? Their existence no longer revolved around planning, as it once had. Now, during every waking instant, they could only cope with the immediate — searching for food and water, keeping warm at night, interacting with nature in the manner of two stray dogs.

Yesterday they had made their way downtown, where they came upon an appliance store. The news was on one of the TVs in the front display window. They saw footage of some California gray whales trapped in the ice of the Arctic Ocean, just off the Alaskan coast. The door of the appliance store had been propped open, and they were able to hear the announcer as he recited the whales' names — Poutu, Siku, and Kannick.

They have names, he had thought, clenching his fists outside the store. We do not. Not anymore. We are just *a couple of homeless people.*

"Come on," she said, pulling at him.

They inched their way out from underneath the Harbor Freeway and began walking in the direction of downtown Los Angeles, less than a mile away. No vehicles were visible overhead, but they could hear the constant swish of traffic, like the formidable workings of some vast air conditioner. He could smell the engine fumes above the odor of their own clothes and bodies.

She paused, then turned and looked back at where they had slept. "It's not such a bad place."

"How can you say that?" he asked, amazed. "It's *dirt.*"

"At least we're not where we used to be."

He assumed she meant the Hollywood Freeway overpass beneath which they had lived until last week. She couldn't have been referring to the Burbank house they had rented so long ago, in that other life. Or was she? Her odd well of hope could suddenly brim so fully, over seemingly nothing, that he wasn't always sure what was going through her mind, or in what context. He had wondered, more than a few times, if she suffered from manic-depressive psychosis. After all, many of the homeless individuals they had met suffered from some sort of mental illness or another.

For a while they had lived below the Hollywood Freeway with a dozen or so other homeless people. The number had constantly changed, as the homeless had come and gone. One night an elderly lady had died in her sleep.

On another night a motorist with a gun had opened fire on them as he ascended a northbound ramp. At least five shots had rung out, and a homeless, nameless, faceless person had been killed. One of society's outcasts. An integral element of absolutely nothing. Slain by what had probably been some drunken or drug-crazed idiot ejaculating his steel manhood out of a car window, for fun.

They continued to descend the dirt slope. Ahead he could see the thin, rust-colored saucer of pollution hanging in the sky over the downtown area. Funny how you didn't notice it when you were directly underneath it.

They walked and walked and walked. So much of life anymore was nothing but walking, a largely pointless moving around of selves. He recalled a time, in that other life, when they had driven, when each of them had owned an automobile. His, a 1979 Oldsmobile Cutlass Supreme; hers, a 1976 Nova. Neither anything fancy; simply vehicles that rolled along, that got the job done.

They had once had jobs too. He had written feature stories for a small daily newspaper in the San Fernando Valley, she had been a hospital secretary. They had met at a dance club, fallen in love, and married. They had moved into a house, splitting the bills. Everything had gone smoothly for one year. Then little chinks in the armor of financial security had begun to manifest themselves.

In a four-month period the Olds required repairs totaling $750. In that same time span their rent jumped from $800 to $850 a month. A statewide drought caused grocery prices to skyrocket. They made one too many foolish purchases with the plastic money. Because of a computer error, her credit union accidentally canceled her account, and by the time she found out what was going on, seventeen checks had bounced, and these worthless pieces of paper came back to them in the mail, accompanied by nearly $300 in overdraft charges. During the month she needed to clear up the confusion regarding the account, the two of them waged four heated arguments, with her slapping him across the face at the end of the final one. He fled the house for five days, wondering about their future together and ringing up $450 in lodging and bar bills while staying at a Santa Monica hotel. He finally returned home, they kissed and made up, and then the $270 phone bill arrived. Turns out that, while he had been moping along the beach those five days, she had called many relatives and friends in distant parts of the country. More arguments. He couldn't take it anymore. He started mouthing off to the wrong

179

people at work and making amateurish mistakes in his reporting. He was fired. She did not miss this opportunity to make him feel useless by saying cruel things to him. More bar bills. Her car began acting up; repairs would cost more than the car was worth. They sold it for $300, hoping that one car would be enough for both of them. But his conked out for good only two months later, and he sold it for its parts for $200. At about that time the landlord came along and demanded his money, inquiring about the conspiracy behind a rubber check he had received. They apologized for having slightly overextended themselves the previous month and gave him the $500 they had collected for the two vehicles plus the additional $350, draining their joint savings account down to less than $100. The landlord left, reasonably satisfied, but they knew the next rent payment was due in three weeks. She got paid in two days, however, so they took that $400 and — after hurriedly selling virtually all their clothes and the VCR and the microwave and the stereo and the television and the answering machine and the music CDs and the videocassette tapes and the personal computer — came up with enough money to cover the next month's rent, with some left over. But he drank some of that, and she got robbed in the parking lot of a grocery store. You'd better find a job quick, she warned him. Then she lost her job. Downsizing. Ha! he said. How does it feel? They had no income. Their lives were evaporating right before their very eyes. They found themselves living in an empty house, empty not only of furnishings but also of any hope for the future. The house became a chilly, shadowy place — literally, because they hadn't been able to pay the last gas and electric bills. The phone had been disconnected as well. At last they found themselves on the street, with only some clothes, a couple of pillows, and a knapsack filled with a few cups, some silverware, handkerchiefs, a razor, and assorted sentimental items.

Such had been the anatomy of their downfall.

They reached the weeds at the bottom of the slope, and his foot bumped against something. He bent over and picked up a paperback book someone had probably thrown from a car while speeding along the freeway. It was a D. H. Lawrence novel, with many passages underlined in red ink. He imagined a college student racing to some drunken orgy after completing his midterm in lit class, flinging the book out of the car, yelling to fellow students riding with him, "No more of that shit!"

He sat down and read some of the highlighted paragraphs. She waited patiently at his side. Presently he began to sob.

"What's wrong?" she asked, sitting down next to him.

"I read this when I was twenty or so," he said, waving the book at her. He leafed through more pages. "I remember some of the sentences. They remind me of whole chapters I read." His shoulders heaved as his head sunk between them. "Nowadays I can't even afford a book. It's like a completely different life. Yet we're the same people. Aren't we?" An intense rage rushed over him, and he flung the book away. "We don't deserve our lives."

"We just had some bad luck," she said. "Things will get better."

He wanted to tell her the "bad luck" had occurred years ago, with nothing getting any better since then, but why depress her? She was trying to do a good deed, trying to lift his spirits.

She got up, helped him to his feet, and urged him on beside her. In seemingly no time at all they were in the city, roaming the streets. Car horns blared. They saw the black exhaust clouds burst from the pipes of the RTD buses as they groaned away from curbs. He was glad to get out of the rough terrain where the weeds grew and onto the easily negotiable cement of the sidewalks. One of his shoes had worn through at a spot on the sole, and it hurt that portion of his foot to step on sharp, unexpected objects; here on the sidewalks, he could more easily observe, and thereby dodge, any pebbles or broken glass or unidentifiable bits of hostile metal that lay ahead of him. He had tried putting a handkerchief in the shoe, over the hole, but after one day of walking with that, his misaligned ankle had ached for a week.

As they proceeded from block to block, they stopped at the webbed trash cans located at the corners of intersections and sifted diligently through the refuse in search of food. They never passed a trash can, not a single one, without pawing through its contents. No piece of garbage went unanalyzed. Most of what they examined was worthless. They knew how pathetic they appeared to the business people briskly marching by in every direction.

They're better than us, he thought. They fit in; they've found a comfortable niche. They go to their offices and earn their paychecks and meet their obligations to society, and after they've done all that, they enjoy their lives. They possess the savvy to do what they need to do.

We, on the other hand, are victims. We don't understand the world. We ran with the pack for a little while, but we couldn't finish the race.

In the fifteenth trash can she discovered a half eaten slice of watermelon. They picked off the tiny black bugs and a white square that looked like an alcohol pad stuck to one side, and they ate what remained. Though they pretended not to notice, they both heard a child call out, "Mom, look at that!"

Four cold French fries and — unbelievably — a plate of two reasonably warm sausages later, he tugged at her arm and, motioning with his head, said, "The appliance store is over here, around the corner."

She stared blankly at him.

"The whales," he explained. "You wanted to see the whales?"

She didn't seem to comprehend his words, but she came along with him anyway. Her morning confusion each day at about this time was partly what made him think she had some sort of psychological problem. Why, all of a sudden, did she want to just stand there, absolutely motionless, gazing off into the distance? He doubted he would ever know.

They arrived outside the appliance store. It was almost noon, the temperature was in the low seventies, and again the door was propped open. Customers streamed in and out of the store, not acknowledging them, even though he pleaded for change on three occasions.

The TV near the entrance was tuned to the usual channel. A game show was almost over.

He placed an arm around her and buried his lips in the hair covering her ear. "The whales will be on in a minute," he whispered.

Silently she looked through the plate glass window at the picture on the TV. A soup commercial was playing.

When the noon newscast came on, an update on the whales was the top story. Nearly three minutes of air time were devoted to the plight of the big mammals.

The baby whale had died. It had banged its head against the eighteen-inch-thick ice so many times, in its attempt to break free, that it had exhausted itself. Bone was exposed on its snout, where it had repeatedly struck the ice.

The two adult whales bobbed up and down in a hole in the ice, coming to the surface for air. Some of the rescuers knelt down at the edge of the hole and petted the whales.

Eskimo teams armed with chain saws were busy cutting new holes, allowing the whales to move closer to the open ocean. Their movement was a good sign, as some scientists had feared the huge creatures might become genetically keyed to remaining in their original hole in order to survive.

The United States was involved in the struggle to save the whales: the National Oceanic and Atmospheric Administration, the Alaska National Guard, and Standard Oil, among others, were helping. The rescue mission was a great public relations opportunity that would have a positive aftereffect, even if it failed.

The California gray whale was not an endangered species, if he remembered correctly from his newspaper days, but international concern for these trapped whales had nevertheless been rampant. The Russians pitched in; their massive icebreakers were punching tirelessly through stubborn pressure ridges.

The Archimedean Screw Tractor, the only mechanical creation of its kind in the world, was cutting a fifteen-foot-wide path in the ice as its aluminum pontoons threaded their way toward the whales.

The two adult whales would live. As he stared at the TV, he was convinced of it. The problem was being addressed, which meant it would be solved.

He was happy for the whales, because that was the decent thing to be. How could you be bitter over such beautiful animals receiving a second chance to live?

He glanced at his wife. She was empty, beyond emotion. Her face was a land-scape of tired bloodlessness.

Turning his attention back to the TV, he watched the whales continue to come up for air. The Eskimos sawed, the scientists gestured, the Archimedean Screw Tractor twisted violently against the ice.

he visualized his wife and himself as the whales. He forgot about trash cans and smelly clothes and locating suitably private places to defecate. He clutched her harder, and her head lolled in his direction. He watched them on TV — his wife and himself. He saw the last chunks of ice split apart and float away as they lunged joyfully out of the water, splashing, leaping, swimming toward better days.

How should we treat a convicted criminal who has served his sentence and is now free if we feel the punishment wasn't severe enough? Here's a story about a town that, underneath its placid veneer, is having trouble coping with that exact dilemma.

SPRAY PAINTING THE SIDE OF THE BARBERSHOP

It was a beautiful July morning, the first day of my two-week vacation, so after eating breakfast and showering, I decided to take a walk before the humidity kicked in.

Wearing my red Speedo shorts, a faded Joe Walsh concert T-shirt from the 1980s, and new Reeboks, I left the house and strolled south on the sidewalk with no particular destination in mind. My Speedos were technically swim trunks, but they doubled nicely as shorts. Their elastic inner webbing gave me room to move, so to speak. I rarely wore socks during the summer, but I sprinkled foot powder in my athletic shoes a couple times a day to prevent sweat and odor.

My watch said 9:50. I'd slept in. Hey, I was on vacation.

I wasn't planning to travel or start any major projects. Mine was a simple lifestyle. I was a relaxed kind of guy, somewhat of a loner, with no current lady involvements. At age forty, I still felt no tremendous urge to get married. Over the next two weeks I planned to rent some movies, drink some beer, watch some NAS-CAR racing, and maybe mow the lawn, depending on how fast the grass grew. Perhaps I would read a few books, but like most people who said they intended to do that on their vacations, I probably wouldn't.

Reggie Hirsch pedaled his bicycle toward me on the street. He was only five feet tall, but his head was bigger than a basketball. He'd been born hydrocephalic, with only sparse hair on the lumpy bulge of his skull. Though in his late twenties, Reggie still lived at home with his parents. Where else was there for him to go? His physical shortcomings kept him from holding down a job, and even if he'd been able to work, he couldn't have lived on his own. To his credit, though, Reggie had calmed down some in recent years, his emotional outbursts occurring less often than when he was a teenager.

I noticed Reggie had pretty well mastered bicycle riding. He'd learned to compensate for the amplified sway of his weighty, fluid-filled noggin by shifting his skinny hips with an eerie shrewdness, keeping his frame in alignment with the bike's. Now if he could only learn to stop at red lights, the motoring townsfolk who knew him or knew of him wouldn't have to take extra care about not running him over when driving through intersections with full right-of-way.

To this day, a sullen handful of Benton, Indiana, residents — mostly old gossips who lived on from one decade to the next, like sturdy oak trees — believed Reggie had killed a boy in 1984. I'd always regarded as ridiculous the idea that he'd strangled twelve-year-old Kyle Shaeffer.

Police discovered Kyle's body late one afternoon in the dirt beneath the jungle gym in the smaller of the town's two parks. No physical evidence connected Reggie to Kyle's death, but a couple people claimed to have seen Reggie lingering near the park at around the time Kyle was determined to have died. This was before Reggie was put on methylphenidate, when he was known to have a volatile temper. But could a wild moodswing have triggered the big-headed boy — given him the strength — to kill Kyle? Merely because Kyle had regularly made fun of him? I doubted it, and so did every other sensible individual. Hell, Kyle had mouthed off to everybody at one time or another, including me. That's the kind of kid he'd been. None of which meant, of course, that he'd deserved to die so brutally.

In any event, the Shaeffers had moved to California more than a decade ago, and for the people of Benton, the horror of Kyle's unsolved murder had dwindled nearly to insignificance, as if it had drifted west in pursuit of the family.

"Hello, Reggie," I said as he sped by me.

"Ga," he squawked, which, for him no doubt, was <u>hi</u> on a good day. He was frowning like usual and never looked up from the road, even when his head lolled at cockeyed angles.

After strolling less than four blocks, I already felt tiny beads of sweat sprouting on my forehead and upper back. Yesterday the temperature had hit 102, and today was threatening to be equally hot. Like hell I'd mow the lawn if this kept up. Luckily the next corner on my route was maple-lined Morehouse Street, where all the trees were huge and leafy. I turned left and exhaled in relief as shade engulfed me.

Bob Brannigan's dog was loose again. Culprit, a handsome Rottweiler, was racing across lawns and between shrubs in my direction. Given his dense build, it was amazing how fast he could run when the urge overtook him. I was familiar with Culprit and knew not to be afraid of him. In defiance of the breed's largely unjustified reputation, he really liked people. He became surly if you <u>didn't</u> pet him. Like most Rottweilers, he demanded lots of attention.

Culprit, with his black-spotted tongue hanging limply from a corner of his smiling mouth, stopped before me, made a very deliberate effort at adjusting his weight, and leapt up, his front paws dragging down across my chest. I rubbed his ears and patted the top of his head — the rougher the better, as far as Culprit was concerned. Then, before he could lose interest in me and race off to the next distraction, I grabbed his collar and, bending at the waist, guided him back the way he had come, in the direction of Bob's house. He went without resistance, gleeful that someone was interacting with him.

Bob lived in the next block. The last time I'd talked to him, about a month ago in the 7-Eleven, he'd told me the county's animal control officer had picked up Culprit three times this year for running loose in the neighborhood. Some of the huge maples on Morehouse were on Bob's property, so I'd asked him, in a mildly sarcastic tone, if he'd ever considered tying Culprit to one of the trees to keep him at home. He'd grinned, those perfect teeth shining within his seemingly permanent tan, and said he'd probably have to resort to some kind of restraining measure, bad as he hated to, if Janet Colby, the pet policewoman, kept picking up Culprit and charging Bob enormous fines for her trouble.

"Last year Culprit ran away a dozen times or more," Bob had informed me, "and Janet never nabbed him once. He always returns home eventually, and it's not like he's going to bite anybody. What's with her?"

I'd refrained from pointing out to Bob that last year he hadn't been screwing Janet's younger married sister — some school teacher I'd never met. More than a few people were aware of it and regarded it as shameful. Personally I couldn't have cared less.

Bob was standing on the front stoop of his single-story house in nothing but light blue boxer shorts, getting yelled at by his neighbor lady to the east. I think her name was Opal, but I wasn't sure. Her fuzzy bathrobe hung to just past her knees. Wicked-looking varicose veins traced the highways of hell upon her lower legs, and her neck was decorated with a raised, fist-size splotch that looked like a cross between bread crust and skin grafting gone bad. Occasionally I saw Opal around town, and judging by the company she kept, I assumed she was one of those gossipy types who loved to ruin reputations by regurgitating hurtful myths about her fellow townspeople and talking about all the things she didn't know.

"Look at my zinnias!" Opal screamed, repeatedly thrusting a finger in the direction of the flowerbed separating her property from Bob's. She stood on a slate path stretching across her lawn to her mailbox. "Look at them! <u>Ruined!</u> All because of that damned stupid dog of yours and his damned big paws. He ran right through them!"

"Hello, Larry," called Bob, seeing me weave down the sidewalk toward him with a lively Culprit in tow.

"There he is," spat Opal, glaring at the dog. "The damned oaf. He ought to be taken out and shot." Then, to Bob: "If you spent as much time keeping an eye on your dog as you do Margie Blackman, he'd never get out of your bedroom."

Apparently Blackman was the married name of Janet Colby's sister. I didn't know the first thing about the Blackmans, nor was I particularly curious. Their sex troubles, and Bob's possible role as a catalyst in them, were their business. Unlike Opal and her immortal ilk, I wasn't a busybody. The Opals of Benton, female and male, dealt with the tears in the town's social fabric by whispering about them to one another, by manufacturing silly, knee-jerk solutions to problems that usually died out on their own, if they were even real to begin with. Hang Reggie Hirsch! Shoot Culprit! Run that slut Margie Blackman out of town! Okay, the murder of Kyle Shaeffer had been a serious matter, as murder by its definition always was, and it would have been nice if someone had been brought to justice for that crime. But even that killing was an event the passage of time had faded to an almost indiscernible gray, stripping away its lurid coating, and why the Opals felt it necessary to continue to badmouth Reggie behind his back, after all these years, was a question I couldn't answer. Without actually trying, I forgot practically everything soon after it happened, as if it were ancient history. When it didn't affect me directly, I remained blissfully insulated. Many things — like Margie Blackman's affair with Bob Brannigan — failed even to register with me. Was this stupidity on my part? Apathy? Good health? My loner's personality?

Without speaking to me, Opal slapped agitatedly at her hairnet as she stomped back inside her house, the screen door creaking shut behind her. I made my way up to Bob and turned Culprit over to him, for which he thanked me. As the dog drooled in the rising heat, Bob and I talked for five or ten minutes about nothing important — the kind of meaningless conversation I enjoyed when on vacation. He vaguely suggested we go fishing together someday on Lake Wawasee, where he kept a pontoon boat, but I couldn't imagine us ever really doing it, since we weren't all that close. So I basically let that ball drop in a moment pregnant with silence.

I resumed my walk. Leaving Morehouse Street behind, I turned onto Beardsley Avenue. The maple trees disappeared with an eerie abruptness. I began changing directions more frequently, at random, taking this street and that, seeing people I knew or at least recognized: Jake Holderman, who'd cleaned out my furnace last fall; Molly Weaver, the librarian; the attractive blonde with the goofy-looking glasses pulling out of her driveway en route to her job at the post office. Eventually I passed by the small, empty park.

(where Kyle Shaeffer was murdered)

and, not fifteen minutes later, found myself strolling past <u>his</u> place. Lance Fleming's house. A brown structure with bug-spattered white shutters on Illinois Street.

(Kyle, Lance, Kyle, Lance)

I was on vacation. I didn't want my mind thinking about Kyle Shaeffer or Lance Fleming. Especially Lance. I honestly hadn't thought about either of them in years. Why was I today? I hadn't meant to venture anywhere near Lance's house, where his mother had dug in and weathered the storm all the while her only son had been in prison. I took frequent walks, whether on vacation or not, but it had been years since I'd ambled down this particular street. Suddenly I became a rusty, awkward automaton as I carefully negotiated the section of sidewalk fronting Lance's place. Each step took a millennium to complete as my body seemed to

190

inflate to twice its normal size. I was glaringly aware of my imagined bigness, of the house to my left seeming like a poised, predatory animal, its largely dark front blocking out the horizon like a behemoth's gaping mouth ready to devour me.

(don't stumble, don't fall down, don't make noise)

The sole of my shoe caught on a small twig in the middle of the sidewalk and dragged it along the cement with a loud scraping sound

(don't make noise, stupid!)

undoubtedly heard throughout the entire neighborhood. Was Lance inside? Was he looking out, looking at me? Thinking ill of me? Lumping me together with everybody else in town? I realized how self-conscious I was in struggling not to turn my head and attempt to peer in through the reflections of light and image that, out of the corner of my eye, I saw lurking in the thick glass of the huge picture window.

Even though the temperature was rapidly rising, a chill zapped my spine, making my shoulders and upper arms tremble.

I escaped the vicinity of Lance's house and decided I was close enough to Benton's main square to stop in at Dan's and get a haircut. My hair wasn't as long as I usually let it grow, but with the heat and humidity coming on strong, I figured a trim, at the very least, would feel good.

A paint spray gun was hissing loudly as I neared Dan's Barbershop. Flush with one side of Dan's building was Yvonne's Drugs. It hadn't been a part of the national Rexall chain for more than twenty years, but no one had ever bothered to take down the faded orange and blue sign that ran across the rooftop. Yvonne McClennan and her husband, Garth, had bought the store ages ago, and since Yvonne was always there, day and night, running the business with untiring hands-on obsessiveness, everybody began calling it Yvonne's Drugs. It was even listed that way in the local phone directory.

On the other side of Dan's, at the southeast corner of Main and First streets, was a weed-choked lot where a dilapidated pickup truck filled with what looked like drop cloths and paint supplies was parked. A hardware store owned by George Stoddard once occupied the lot; it had burned down twelve winters ago. Afterward George had erected a larger, more modern hardware five miles outside of town so that many of the area's farmers, who gave him the majority of his business, wouldn't have so far to drive. George still owned the empty lot and had never appeared interested in doing anything productive with it, including selling it. The Opals of Benton sometimes whispered that George had started the blaze himself to collect a bunch of insurance money so he could afford to relocate.

A man in green slacks and a white, short-sleeved shirt stood in the abandoned lot beside the fellow who was operating the spray gun. I didn't know them. The heavyset guy in green slacks had his back to me, gazing at the barbershop's north wall, his pudgy, raised arms making windshield wiper motions above his head. The other man, whom I could sometimes see slightly from the side as he moved about, was bald and wore a white mask that covered most of his face. He was closer to the barbershop, and his torso swiveled left and right while he shuffled sideways inches at a time, toward Main, spraying a coat of gray paint on the ancient cement blocks comprising Dan's exposed side wall. Thistles and milkweed plants fluttered against the men's ankles and knees in the glaring morning light.

Black and red graffiti had been painted all over the wall, probably during the night just ended. Now the spray gun operator was covering the graffiti. An UCK U! disappeared beneath a shower of gray. I didn't need a Ph.D. degree to deduce what the first word had been. Some turbulently rendered geometric shapes, along with an exaggerated penis with testicles attached, were next to recede in a bland mist.

Graffiti was not a common sight in Benton but, like most of a town's difficulties, could be easily dealt with and soon forgotten. A masked man had arrived to save the day! If a Janet Colby type had been present, maybe she could have fined someone. Nobody had really murdered Kyle Shaeffer, if in fact there'd ever been a murder at all.

(Lance Fleming could've done it; there's a 2 + 2 nobody ever tried to add up)

The Opals in town would learn of the defacement of Dan's wall and prattle about it for weeks to come, to the benefit of no one.

As I approached the two men from behind, I realized I *did* know the one in the green slacks: it was Dan himself, my barber for as long as I could remember. I was used to seeing him inside the shop, moving in a slower, more controlled fashion — especially his arms. And I couldn't honestly say I'd ever paid any attention to his pants.

"God damn kids," Dan barked, his comment seeming to go unnoticed by the busy painter. "Why the hell don't their parents keep track of them?"

"Dan!" I called, trying to sound cheery.

He spun around, beads of perspiration flying off his bristly brow, and said, "Hello, Larry. You working banker's hours these days?"

I explained I was on vacation. Above the persistent hiss of the spray gun, Dan cursed Benton's adolescent population some more, gesturing in frustration at his violated wall, as if I'd have been unable to see it without his guidance. His eyebrows glistened beneath the morning sun. You couldn't ignore them: as overgrown as the weedy lot in which we stood, they weren't just thick, they were long and strangely arced, curling downward like an extra set of eyelashes. They were like a mild genetic mutation — Reggie Hirsch

(there's Reggie, evil child strangler, seeping up out of the gray matter again)

on a minuscule scale. Odd that Dan never appeared to clip them, considering he was a barber. Maybe he was proud of them.

"You want a haircut?"

I nodded. "But it can wait, if you're busy with — "

"Come on," he said, waving for me to follow him. "I just opened up an hour ago. God damn kids." As we walked away from the painter, Dan waved at him and wagged a thumb toward the doorway of his shop. The bald head, sweat- and paint-speckled above the peculiar-looking mask, nodded in comprehension. Its owner looked like an alien from a cheap 1950s science fiction film. The mask filtered out the harmful gases of Earth's atmosphere. His paint gun was a death ray, and his race had traveled light-years to destroy humanity.

We strolled into the otherwise unoccupied barbershop, both of us stepping over the dirty metal threshold, which I knew as well as Dan was loose and made a loud clattery sound if a foot connected with it in just the wrong way. If Dan ever found himself in the mood to cut his eyebrows, maybe he'd also take a screwdriver and fasten down that broad sill.

As usual during the warm months, Dan's door was propped wide open. He was allergic to air conditioning, I'd heard him tell curious patrons. A fan stirred lazily and quietly in the far corner. The blinds in the twin front windows were closed at the top, halving the rectangles of sunshine on the linoleum floor. Eight chairs for potential waiting customers lined a wall. Tiny white tables interspersed among them were strewn with magazines and newspapers.

Dan dabbed his wet forehead with a towel. As he talked about being awakened that morning by a phone call from Lottie Proctor, one of the Opals, in which he learned of the vandalism to his building, I climbed into the barber chair, closed my eyes, and let him drape the striped sheet over my body.

"The usual?" he asked me.

"Yeah," I said. "That's fine."

Standing behind me, Dan gave my hair a fresh combing, clicked on his electric clippers, and started cutting. He asked me how I planned to spend my vacation. I asked him if he'd sold his Buick yet. After a time the spray gun outside sputtered into silence, and I heard the man toss it into the back of the pickup, on top of one of the drop cloths, with a dull thud. No further noise came from the empty lot. Maybe the painter was doing some final work on Dan's wall with a brush, or maybe he'd walked down the street to the Benton Home Style Cafe for a cup of coffee.

Dan said he and his wife were planning to take a vacation of their own in September. "Yeah, we always enjoy Vegas, so we're gonna — "

He paused, snapped off the clippers abruptly. I thought about opening my eyes to see who was lingering in the open doorway. Someone was there, because even from behind closed eyelids, I sensed that the light entering the shop from out of a cloudless sky had diminished.

(the painter?)

"Get out of here," said Dan as he moved to the side of the barber chair. A chilly, ruffled Dan, making me uneasy. A primal, seething rage boiling up out of his gut and searing his speech. Causing my neck hairs to prickle and waves of adrenaline to pulse through me.

"Sorry to see what happened to your — "

"I don't care! Get lost!"

Lance Fleming — I'd recognized his voice — uttered not another word as he removed himself from the barbershop doorway and, judging by the sound of his footsteps, headed down the sidewalk in the direction of Yvonne's. He wouldn't be allowed in there either.

Fleming hadn't said, "Hi, Larry, how ya doin'?" or anything else to that effect; he'd given up on that sort of feeble stab at an exchange with me two or three years back.

Unlike how he'd reacted to the nameless culprits who had painted obscenities on his wall, Dan didn't anguish over Fleming's unexpected arrival, after the fact, with a "God damn pervert" or anything else. For my ten remaining minutes in the shop, which gradually assumed the aspect of an eternity, not another word was said, by either of us, about Benton's most despised felon. Not another word was said, period, until after Dan finished giving me my haircut, and I asked him how much I owed him, and he mumbled ten dollars.

I left the barbershop. The painter had removed his mask and was sitting on the open tailgate of his truck, smoking a cigarette and staring off into the distance. His nose was almost more unsightly than the mask had been — oddly angled, lumpy, threatening to displace his upper lip.

Fleming was nowhere in sight, for which I was grateful.

A Benton native, Fleming had been sent to prison in Indianapolis fourteen years ago, at age twenty-six, for doing abusive and illegal sexual things to a child.

(a year after Kyle Shaeffer was found dead)

He'd been sentenced to twenty-five years but had served only nine. All during the trial, and ever since, he'd maintained his innocence.

Fleming's mother, Jane, had become a Benton pariah in her own right, thanks to her son. Shunned, whispered about by the Opals as well as many folks who weren't necessarily full-time Opals, she'd continued to live in the same house on Illinois Street after the molester had gone to jail. Fleming's dad had died of liver failure years earlier. As an adult, Fleming had lived alone with his mother up until the time he'd been sent away.

After his release from prison in 1994, Fleming had returned to Benton and his old house. It was still in his mother's name, but she no longer lived there; she was in a nursing home in Lafayette, sick with cancer.

No family members or friends anchored Fleming to Benton, because he had none of either here. Rumor had it he'd come back to his old, familiar town purely as a demonstration of his innocence. He wasn't going to be run out of town on a rail for something he hadn't done, by God!

People dealt with problems in a variety of ways. They handed out fines. They gossiped. They spray painted over them. Or, like the Shaeffer family, they moved on.

But what did a community do when one of its own members was himself a problem perceived as so serious that no solution seemed workable? When it wasn't just the deed done — having an affair, spreading graffiti, even committing a murder — but rather the person himself? How to cope with a man's sick nature? His warped thoughts, his twisted desires, the dark interstices of his mind? What could be done to an individual who, according to the state at least, had paid his debt to society and therefore couldn't be fined or officially penalized any further, even if it didn't feel like it was enough? What if his transgression — the problem he'd not only caused but still embodied — was so unspeakable that even the Opals fell silent? What could be done when that person did not, physically, *go away?*

That person, in effect, disappeared in another way. As much as possible, no one talked to him, no one did business with him, because he wasn't actually there. And no one — not even the Opals — talked *about* him. That person had to drive all the way to Lafayette not only to see his ailing mother but also to get a haircut.

I'd never fished with the philandering Bob Brannigan, but Fleming and I had spent a lot of hours casting lines together when we were kids. We were in the same high school graduating class. He'd once shown me his vast collection of comic books.

I hadn't visited, spoken to, or hung out with Fleming since his return to Benton more than half a decade ago. Sometimes I felt guilty about that, but then again, not.

Walking back home from Dan's Barbershop, I once more found myself on Illinois Street, approaching Fleming's house, pausing directly in front of it. I turned and faced it. The heat was relentless. My backbone was an icicle. New sweat gushed from me. I needed a drink. Sunlight reflected off of Fleming's big window more relentlessly than before, shielding the living room. Was Fleming in there? If so, what was he looking at? What was he *doing?*

(Christ, I'm turning into an Opal!)

I wondered about proceeding up the walk, knocking on the door, and saying hi, but I finally decided against that plan.

No one was inside anyway. It was an empty house.

About The Author

Kent Robinson is the author of dozens of short stories in a wide variety of genres, including contemporary, horror, mystery and suspense, and science fiction and fantasy. A former newspaper reporter, he served as news writer for the University of Southern California (USC) for nine years, during which time a LexisNexis search determined him to be the most prolific press release writer of any college or university in the United States. (He wrote more than five thousand altogether.) He holds a journalism degree from Franklin College and is an affiliate member of the international Horror Writers Association.

Printed in the United States
23346LVS00001B/119